Images of Elsewhere

Images of Elsewhere

Vol. VI

PETER LANG

Oxford - Berlin - Bruxelles - Chennai - Lausanne - New York

Images of Elsewhere

Timothy Jenkins

PETER LANG
Oxford · Berlin · Bruxelles · Chennai · Lausanne · New York

Bibliographic information published by the Deutsche Nationalbibliothek.
The German National Library lists this publication in the German National Bibliography;
detailed bibliographic data is available on the Internet at http://dnb.d-nb.de.

A catalogue record for this book is available from the British Library.

Library of Congress Cataloging-in-Publication Data

Names: Jenkins, Timothy, 1952- author.
Title: Images of elsewhere / Timothy Jenkins.
Other titles: Images of elsewhere (Book)
Description: Oxford ; Bern ; Berlin ; Bruxelles ; New York ; Wien : Peter
   Lang, [2025] | Series: Images of elsewhere ; vol. VI (6) | Includes
   bibliographical references and index.
Identifiers: LCCN 2024035328 (print) | LCCN 2024035329 (ebook) | ISBN
   9781803741611 (paperback) | ISBN 9781803741628 (ebook) | ISBN
   9781803741635 (epub)
Subjects: LCSH: Unidentified flying objects--History. | Unidentified flying
   objects--Philosophy.
Classification: LCC TL789 .J4635 2025 (print) | LCC TL789 (ebook) | DDC
   001.942--dc23/eng20240809
LC record available at https://lccn.loc.gov/2024035328
LC ebook record available at https://lccn.loc.gov/2024035329

Cover image: Line drawing by the author.
Cover design by Peter Lang Group AG

ISBN 978-1-80374-161-1 (print)
ISBN 978-1-80374-162-8 (ePDF)
ISBN 978-1-80374-163-5 (ePub)
DOI 10.3726/b20805

© 2025 Peter Lang Group AG, Lausanne
Published by Peter Lang Ltd, Oxford, United Kingdom
info@peterlang.com - www.peterlang.com

Timothy Jenkins has asserted his right under the Copyright, Designs and Patents Act, 1988,
to be identified as Author of this Work.

All rights reserved.
All parts of this publication are protected by copyright.
Any utilisation outside the strict limits of the copyright law, without the permission of the
publisher, is forbidden and liable to prosecution.
This applies in particular to reproductions, translations, microfilming, and storage and processing
in electronic retrieval systems.

This publication has been peer reviewed.

Contents

Series Preface — vii

Acknowledgement — xi

Introduction — 1

CHAPTER 1
A spectrum of scientific models — 9

CHAPTER 2
Sightings and reports — 25

CHAPTER 3
Images of elsewhere — 87

Bibliography — 115

Personal acknowledgements — 119

Index — 121

Series Preface

Reports of flying saucers – also known as UFOs – constitute a puzzle, for they are numerous, well attested, and hard to believe. There are tempting shortcuts to a 'solution' – that the sightings are real, or mistaken, or fictitious (made up) – but none of these prove satisfactory. Instead, we are brought to consider the history of sightings and the history, also, of how it became possible to regard such incidents in the terms that have become customary. Flying saucers in this fashion become a feature of the wider society, and allow an angle of approach to our modern, technological civilization: a small-scale problem that allows insight into the larger setting.

The six essays stand as independent studies. Each deals with an aspect of the life of flying saucers or UFOs: their appearance after the Second World War within the constellation of military and technological interests, their debt to early science fiction and its sources, the development of the search for signs of extra-terrestrial intelligence, the first adoptions of the 'interplanetary hypothesis' in civilian circles, the further expansion of reports, first, of sightings and, then, of abductions in the wider society, and, finally, a review of the range of forms which have appeared. Taken together, they form a thorough enquiry into reports of sightings of flying saucers.

The series as a whole makes three contributions to resolving the puzzle posed by such reports.

First, it relates three bodies of materials from the United States in the mid-twentieth century whose interactions must be taken into consideration when speaking about flying saucers. These are the science fiction milieu, the interplay of military and technical interests, and reports of sightings by members of the public; in short, stories, military work, and ordinary lives. The first contribution is to study their interactions, overlaps, borrowings and synergies.

The second is to derive the categories that are necessary to explain the convergence of these materials. Repeating patterns appear in science fiction literature, the history of Air Force intelligence in the Cold War period, the early days of NASA, the search for extra-terrestrial intelligence, and a wide variety of incidents and claims made by members of the public. To make sense of their common nature and to see how their interactions work, we also need to investigate some intellectual history. There is a longstanding tradition of popular thought putting new scientific discoveries and technological innovation to work for human moral purposes. This tradition was taken up by military and technical interests in the middle third of the twentieth century, using three clusters of ideas: the intimate connection between military technology and the world picture offered by modern media, the concept of 'communication' (and, post-War, of 'information') that became central in the period, and an understanding of 'memory' as an exact record of the past. These ideas were shared with a wider public: in the context of international tensions, hopes of communication and fears of its breakdown were given expression in the appearance of new forms of life, forms given content by the earlier longstanding history. This is the second contribution the essay makes to the topic: an investigation of the common patterns of thought necessary for stories, military work and ordinary lives to interact.

And, last, a mechanism is proposed by which these interactions occur. This is an analysis of the ways in which these 'images', which contain both real and imaginary elements, make their appearance compelling. I find well documented instances – in particular, the sessions in which memories of abductions are recovered – where the social mechanism is uncovered that allows the oscillation between the two elements, a mechanism that can be glimpsed at work in other sites but which cannot be tracked in such detail in the documents and other sources we have concerning advances in research, security decisions, the records of incidents and so forth. This is the third contribution.

I first came to the puzzle of flying saucer reports when working on spirit messages and similar forms of social life (such as parapsychology and psychical research) and realized that the search for extra-terrestrial intelligence was the latest expression of a long-held desire for communication with disembodied minds compatible with our own. It has taken a good deal of time and work to give substance to this insight. As will be clear from my references, there is an abundance of work of the highest quality in this broad area, on which I draw to give shape to the argument. If I have contributed anything, it is by making a systematic enquiry and by putting together materials that are not always associated, and by continuing to ask questions rather than settling for accepted answers. In this fashion, I hope to have supported readers who find these topics interesting rather than those who wish to close them down, and I also hope to have contributed in some small degree to understanding the contemporary world.

Acknowledgement

Some paragraphs in Chapter 3, concerning recent sightings, appeared as an article, 'It came from outer space', on the Engelsberg Ideas website in July 2021, which was later published in the book *Man and Technology: How Humanity Thrives in a Changing World*, edited by Kurt Almqvist, Alastair Benn and Mattias Hessérus, Axel and Margaret Ax:son Johnson Foundation, 2022: 95–100. The material is used here with permission, which is gratefully acknowledged.

Introduction

Consider three distinct events. First, one night in July 1952, radar systems around Washington, DC, picked up unidentified craft which appeared to fly over the White House and the Capitol. A week later, a repeat incident generated sufficient civilian calls to block Air Force communications for several hours; this was recognized as a security issue, prompting an investigation, at the behest of the President, by the Central Intelligence Agency (CIA). Second, the film *Close Encounters of the Third Kind*, directed by Steven Spielberg, was released by Columbia Pictures in December 1977, and was watched by millions in the following months. Third, in June 2021, the Office of the Director of National Intelligence released a preliminary report on 'Unidentified Aerial Phenomena' (UAPs). This has been followed by a series of congressional hearings. In short, a communications breakdown, the cinema sensation of 1978, a recent government report. What do these events have in common? And how did we get here?

The answer to the first question is flying saucers. There have been reports of sightings of flying saucers for the last eighty years. The term UFO (Unidentified Flying Object) was introduced in the mid-1950s; lately, they have been called UAPs (Unidentified Aerial Phenomena, now, Unidentified Anomalous Phenomena).[1] Both sightings and reports raise questions of what has been seen, on the one hand, and of how it has been spoken of, on the other. In either case, resolving the question is not a simple matter. We can combine the two sets of issues and call the product an 'image', a combination of new things and new ways of conceiving these things.

And how did we get here? There is a history of these images, and the local stages and circumstances of each twist of the tale can be followed. We can trace the origins of the images, or where they have been drawn from, and their first mobilization, starting with small scale concerns within Air Force intelligence in the context of the Cold War. They rapidly escaped

---

1   The last term was introduced by NASA in December 2022.

into the civilian zone and, from these small beginnings, travelled out far into space, with the Search for Extra-Terrestrial Intelligence, and, in contrast, into the lives and concerns of the public, taking many forms, not only Close Encounters and abductions, but also, an increasing presence in advertising and speculation and storytelling in the media, including film.

Yet, this is not a single history with an overall plot we can grasp. There are, rather, multiple paths and connections, transfers and singularities, with no overarching explanation; the images are put to work in different contexts, both taking up elements from and reflecting upon various contingencies. In particular, they respond to changing political moments – the Cold War and, later, tapering off of the Cold War with the end of the Soviet Union – and, equally, to technical innovations, including new forms of communication. In a phrase, the images are principally the product of defence concerns and new media and the technologies associated with each, but there is no overall rationale.

At the same time and in each local setting, there are recurring patterns of how people make sense of these images; there are explanations offered which come down to one of three basic claims: that such sightings occur as described and the reports are true, or that the sightings and reports are mistaken, and so people are deceived, or, third, that the reports are made up and that the sightings never happened. There are refinements possible, but the three proposals concerning the intelligibility of the images are truth, error, or fiction.

It is hard to get past each of these exclusive claims, yet none can be supported reliably without remainder. And the images with which we are concerned only appear in these contradictory claims which, therefore, taken together, constitute the primary materials for research on the topic. In the essays preceding this one, I have reviewed this history in terms of its multiple pathways, the patterns that are exchanged between different parties, the recurrent intellectual models that have been used, and the various practices that underlie these patterns, exchanges and forms.[2] Each essay has been written to stand alone, as a monograph; I examine a series

2   These essays are *Flying Saucers: An Introduction, Religion and Science Fiction, Martian Linguistics, UFO Reports*, and *Alien Sightings*.

of specific problems, tracing the genealogy of the image and exploring the series of texts in which it was given shape, reading the sources in Theosophy and science fiction that created the ground-rules it follows, sketching its birth pangs in the military world and seeing how it has been put to work subsequently in a variety of circumstances, and showing something of the mechanism by which local circumstances and continuing elements are repeatedly assembled together, giving renewed life and force of conviction to the image with all its ambiguities in each repetition.

I offer a summary of these findings in the third chapter, outlining the argument that has emerged from the other essays. The summary can be read independently, but the claims offered are established in the earlier essays. The thesis is that, in the modern period, with understandings shaped by new technologies, we are bound to find something like flying saucers, with properties that are both real and imaginary, which act as relays between human groups, places, and times, providing new resources and allowing innovation to happen. I then consider the approach used that supports this argument and the structuring theme, the contrast between realism and imagination, together with further ideas concerning language, time, and action which persist throughout the series. And I conclude by making a number of more general observations.

Change and time

Before making a summary, however, there is a further question to be asked. It concerns the nature of the phenomenon in its broadest aspect. When the image of the flying saucer first emerged, it was blurred and ill-defined, and it became progressively better-defined, like a photograph being developed (already an old simile); the image became resolved. We can, then, call the problem to be solved 'changes in the presuppositions of everyday thought', corresponding to this appearance, development and resolution. If we have identified the kinds of thinking involved in sighting UFOs and the making of reports, under what conditions do these images appear and have their effects, and how do these conditions evolve? In other words, is there a sociological explanation for the appearances (and disappearances) that concern us and is there some sort of rationale to the shifts in focus of the descriptions offered?

If the topic is *change*, it concerns, as I have emphasized, both the appearance of new objects and alteration in the categories by which we make sense of them. The two are simultaneous and that simultaneity constitutes the difficulty of grasping any innovation. The error of common sense under these conditions is to assume that categories do not change, and so treats new things within existing classes of ideas. Yet, life is not so simple; categories mutate at certain points, and the effects of these alterations work out at different scales: the objects seen, the people who report them, the groups who receive the reports, the experts who debate the terms in which the reports should be construed, the question of what resources should be deployed, and so forth.

In the case in hand, the change with which we are concerned can be put in these terms: in the early 1940s, nobody spoke about flying saucers. Yet, by 1952, they could cause a major threat to military channels of communication, the function of which was vital in case of a surprise attack. By 1978, as UFOs, they could fill cinemas; the population at large could handle the idea without reflection. And by 2021, as UAPs, they had become sufficiently commonplace – though still mysterious – to be the subject of extended government report and debate.

The idea of change, by its nature, implies the topic of time, for it deals with both continuities and discontinuities. The notion of a novelty demands a break with existing habits and traditional ways of seeing things and, sometimes, radical revision of existing explanatory schemas. Confronted in this way, the normal practice – the common-sense practice – is to focus upon novelty and to leave aside questions of continuities. Yet, there are continuities to be discovered, even in the generation and reception of novelty. In this regard, a claim of this research is that a major piece of scaffolding in the history we are telling concerns what can be called liberal Protestant ways of making sense, making sense being considered both actively, as ways of intervening in the world, and passively, as ways of making the world intelligible. What are its characteristics?

The Protestant frame of mind has been described since Weber in terms of a practical, this-worldly, focus, replacing a sacramental or magical understanding of the world. The point of the contrast is to highlight the new combination of practical investigation, seeking to understand the mechanism of how things work, with certain practices of record-keeping and accountability. This association can be linked to the contemporary scientific revolution, with its attitude to nature, and to the practices of capitalism and the development of productive technologies; it correlates too with new political and social ideologies and with new forms of piety, around the notion of the individual and the formation of the autonomous self. Liberal Protestantism is a later variant, born in the nineteenth century, with a particular emphasis on personal responsibility and the consequences of one's actions at every level – hence, reform in the person, marriage, the family, the social order, business, and the place of the human in the natural world. In these essays, these later attitudes have emerged repeatedly in the role played by Spiritualism and its variants, in particular with their interactions with advances in scientific understanding and the accompanying technologies.

Yet, the contrast between Protestant and Catholic, this-worldly and sacramental, pragmatic and magical, is only a shorthand. For the point is that the discontinuities or revolutions in thought that concern us may be thought of in terms of repeated recourse to the resources Protestant thought gives to minorities faced with powerful and authoritarian majorities. That is, the initial recourse to such thinking is to restore a sacramental, immediately engaged, experience of the world: precisely, to renew the heavens and the earth. It may give way to the pragmatic, disciplined, inquisitive attitude to the world which is inherent in the resources, but that is not the initial impulse. The impulse of the Protestant revolution at every iteration is to learn to pray anew, we might say; it is a pious impulse – even if, quickly, its intellectual resources allow the distancing which asks, 'what does praying achieve?', and thinking in terms not of praying but of 'religious experience'.

We can use that analytic mode to ask, what purpose does reaching for such categories serve? As I have suggested, it serves to create a space for a minority, at whatever scale, to live in, defining boundaries, shoring up community and identifying enemies. It creates markers. This is important, because although new explanations are proposed, new mechanisms sought, new forms of intelligibility tried out, the issue of the ultimate persuasiveness or plausibility of the new ideas is less significant than the work done in creating an identity. This is the kind of thinking that serves the claims we have been considering; it creates resources for small acts of renewal, on the basis of which the claimants can act differently in the world.

These two aspects – of living fully in the passing instant, on the one hand, and privileging knowledge and conscious intelligence, on the other – are intimately connected. But the latter continually replaces the former, so that we try to explain things in a new light, interpret phenomena in terms other than the perceptions we have, seek for signs and the active presence of the past (in terms of memories), rather than speak in terms of learning to live faithfully and truthfully, summed up as 'sacramentally'. Yet both impulses are present; there is a continual oscillation between reaching for new possibilities – seeing new things – and the outworking of the accompanying categories, which then gives grounds for investigators to demand explanations, seeking to make the new intelligible, and deciding whether what has been claimed is true, or false, or fiction.

To put it another way, since the idea bears repeating, small groups use the resources to hand, which are liberal Protestant in origin, to find new ways of living 'faithfully and truthfully'. But the resources bear within themselves specific modern means for recovering and covering over this breaking free, by asking what do these activities mean, how are we to interpret them, what lies behind the reaching for new forms of life?

There is then a complex pattern, a recurrent dynamic by which change occurs, by which continuing resources, under the appropriate circumstances, generate new things, both new things and new ways of apprehending them. In sum, when we are considering reports of sightings of flying saucers, the resources represented by liberal Protestant thought are significant – more so than recourse directly to scientific thought or to notions of individual autonomy – and serve repeatedly in the course of the argument. We may conclude that, despite their appearance in the late 1940s, flying saucers were not as new as they appeared to be for, in many regards, they are earlier forms transformed.

Ideas of change, then, necessarily translate into discussions of time and the return of past ideas in present, lively form. The notion of time plays out in concepts of experience and memory or, in the terms of this essay, sighting (visibility) and report. And the two concepts change one into the other and back, for experience is rapidly subsumed under report and yet reappears under the heading of forgetfulness, focussed in the accounts of abduction, which is constructed around the impossibility of remembering and the business of recovering memories and restoring lost time.

The first two chapters

The most general way of grasping this double form of innovation and interpretation, where the second movement appears to cancel the first, is as a process of 'making sense', both in terms of manufacture and description. In sum, if we ask, 'what is going on with the appearance of flying saucers?', the answer will involve change and time and, therefore, discontinuities and continuities, and the business of how experience turns into memory and report. Giving a description of this broad process is the concern of the first two chapters. Here, I use arguments by two twentieth-century philosophers, Gaston Bachelard and Gilles Deleuze, to make sense of the interplay between new objects and new categories and so with the emergence and condensation of the images that are our business. For the one author makes the hardness of the sciences, and the other the hardness of experience, melt; they each point to what we might call the liquid nature of the world and to the trap of believing the world to be solid, measurable, and unable to help us think.

I first review the range of ways of making sense of sightings that have emerged, each of which echoes a distinct scientific style of approach. For contemporary scientific models provide different criteria for understanding the basic nature of the world, and these have all in turn been used to make sense of flying saucers. These ways come under five headings although, since they overlap, there could be other ways of dividing up the spectrum. This is the work of the first chapter, which draws on an essay by Bachelard.

Then, from this survey it emerges there are two major modes for ordering experience and making sense, schemes which serve as the two ends of the spectrum, one focussed on action in the present moment, the other on observation and making descriptions in a more complex temporal setting. This is the business of the second chapter, which explores an argument from Deleuze. There, I outline these two schemes and, in particular, the second, for it allows us to understand a good deal of the more extravagant behaviour and claims which have been our concern. Within this account, the recovery of hidden memories of abduction permits the tracking in some detail of the mechanics of the oscillation between the two schemes, realistic and imaginative, allowing us to perceive the work recovered memory does. This in turn offers sight of the kind of minimal unit required to create more generally the features, puzzles, anomalies, and paradoxes of flying saucer reports.

In short, there are two ways of telling the story of our investigation of a specific history concerning the emergence of flying saucers: on the one hand, a process mirroring the evolution of scientific models, on the other, the increasing complexification of time and with it the implication of the observer in the action. The second is a version of the first.

It must be emphasized that in making this survey, while stepping back from the detailed descriptions on which it depends and considering the qualities that emerge in a more abstract light, we are not abandoning the perspectives provided by the subjects of the enquiry. The claim, rather, is that the categories being explored and the resources they bring belong to those being investigated and are not imported nor imposed by the analysis. We are dealing in the implications of indigenous practices of thought and action.

The essay then introduces new ideas, offering a different and more general understanding of the materials described in earlier essays. While I name specific actors and situations to illustrate the argument – or, better, to draw the argument out from this evidence – I have not included detailed reference back to specific essays; the argument stands in its own terms.

CHAPTER I

A spectrum of scientific models

Before starting, a remark on how the method adopted and the object of study relate. To make comparisons successfully, one needs a well-defined variable and to be able to trace this object through at least three instances. In a sociological study, the object is, in one form or another, the constraints experienced collectively by the subjects, that is, the presuppositions that define what is the case for those subjects, where boundaries lie and what is allowed and what prohibited, what may be thought about and chosen (the permissive) and what may not or is simply given (the prescriptive). We are dealing, then, not in conscious matters, to which the subjects can testify, but in the unconscious, the categories, orderings and values which are taken for granted in any testimony. These presuppositions take many forms. A sociologist therefore does not set out from ideas but from an analysis of the senses, from the human experience of constraint, which is always specific, and so from the conventions and institutions – the social practices – which underwrite this experience.

Such an object of analysis does not remain constant, but under certain conditions mutates. In general, it changes when the simplest social units, persons or small groups, are brought together at different scales. When looking at appearances made by flying saucers, we concentrate for the most part on moments when quite large scale ways of making sense have broken down in some regard, and so when a move has been made from a larger to a smaller scale of organization, allowing initiative to emerge in the smaller units. Moves in the reverse direction can also occur, when the power of initiative moves up a level or more, and this is more or less a given in periods of recovery, when 'normal' conditions are restored. But such moves can also involve radical change. These shifts in scale can be thought of as decisive moments or events, when the size of social group making sense changes along with the accompanying rules and conventions. The task of comparison is to map these decisive moments, creating a scale of forms around a single variable.

The readiest axis for such comparison is then an increase from few to many or decrease from many to few, the consolidation or separation of simple units, leading to new social amalgams with appropriate properties, both intellectual and practical. But one should not imagine such a move is straightforwardly from a small simple state to a large complicated one, marked by independence of the units in question at one end and their interdependence at the other. In practice, complexity is more than a matter of numbers, for beyond the number of social units and the size of populations involved, we also have to take into account the question of the density of moral ties, the relationships that bind and distinguish those participating. Often, the smaller the human scale, the more the group in question gain control over their idiosyncratic productions. The variable to be found in the range of instances is not then to be related precisely to the numbers involved and the correlated complexity of social organization necessary to that scale of operation, but rather to whether the various social institutions, categories and so forth overlap considerably and are shared by component groups or whether, on the contrary, they are dispersed and allow the groups to operate independently of one another in certain regards. These conditions can vary enormously.

To repeat the point, we are dealing with cases where, momentarily, complex overlapping categories and social institutions lose their coherence and force of conviction and so both the scale of effective action diminishes and the autonomy of idiosyncratic categories increases, so that new deals and correspondences emerge. In brief, the variable which concerns the presuppositions we follow is that of social dispersal, with its implied diminution of scale and independence of perception.

In such moments, a newly associated group will borrow ideas from the surrounding environment through which to express their new perceptions. Often, the ideas are taken over because they originate in some regard in the disturbances to basic categories that are being made sense of and which permit the new association. In the cases with which we are concerned, the groups pick up new ideas as to the nature of the real, both new conceptions of the basic conditions of reality and an understanding that our perception of reality will have changed. And these conceptions and this understanding were recast repeatedly by advances in the sciences during the first part of the twentieth century.

One further point: the claim is that, if we go to the smallest possible scale, to the simplest unit, the underlying constraints will appear clearly. Durkheim calls these 'elementary forms'. In this instance, the smallest complete social units are found, as we shall see in Chapter 2, in the therapeutic sessions that recover memories of abductions, and they allow us to see the constructions being used, particularly those relating to time, constructions that are echoed elsewhere in reports of sightings and make intelligible the various more widely shared phenomena. In short, as the scale is reduced, idiosyncratic forms appear that, nevertheless, also reveal the basic mechanisms at work.

I. What counts as real

In this chapter, I characterize the range of styles or sets of presuppositions used in the reports of flying saucers and draw attention to the parallels they make with scientific reports. In terms of the overall history of sightings, we begin by considering the genealogy of the idea of life in space (found in science fiction) and then turn to the production of space craft in security and other official circles, before considering how the public responded to these 'images of life elsewhere' – flying saucers, discs, interplanetary craft, unidentified flying objects, alien messages and so forth. What sense can we make of these images' reception and employment by a wider public once they had been conceived and hatched?

A first observation: as suggested above, a lot depends on the scale of the human unit being considered. Sightings play a role or a range of roles in certain private lives, and it is a recurrent task to try and discern those roles, the uses to which 'seeing' flying saucers have been put. It is possible to pursue, though only in outline because the reported materials are usually very thin, a trio of activities such as the creation of a power of action in the world by commitment to an unorthodox perspective, education in that perspective, and the living out of the practical consequences of this world view.[1] The least one can say is that lives have been changed through an encounter with a flying saucer: new resources found, repairs to past damage attempted, new connections made and former relations cut off.

We move to a larger scale, however, or series of scales, when we consider the reports that emerge from these activities of self-making. For sightings are subject to extensive reporting and hence to disputes of interpretation. Reports involve different sizes of human groups; we find the initial report of a sighting set in a constellation of lives, the spread of such a report, the emergence of interested parties, the various explanations canvassed, the taking of sides and the spread of controversy, sometimes to a national or even international level. Distinctions can be made between core members of these interested groups, their immediate followers and the wider audiences who take an interest, and we should also include the yet-wider circles of casual readers and viewers to whom these matters make some kind of sense. And we find records actively employed and produced in every part of the process: inscriptions and signs, letters, books consulted, and published reports – from newsletters to national journals, for different kinds of readers – not to mention amateur photographs and moving film, which have, however, played a more minor role as evidence than might have been expected. These materials are then repeated and transformed in various guises, in magazines, television programmes and series, a variety of films, and spread on the Internet.

This distinction between sightings and reports, between, we might say, visual and linguistic images, may be borne in mind in the following discussion, although much of the time, sightings vanish into reports: the truly small scale is quickly lost sight of.

---

1   Faubion labels the three elements 'conversion', 'gnosis' and 'ethical self-cultivation', together comprising an analysis of 'the dynamics of religious commitment' (Faubion 2001: xvii).

Styles of explanation

If we focus on reports, the point to notice at the outset is that the reports of all kinds use a range of explanatory presuppositions, and that these presuppositions are borrowed from, or have their parallels in, natural scientific schemes of thought. That is, each report assumes a certain account of the natural and physical world, and these accounts can vary radically one from another. We can identify five types or styles of explanation, distinguished by the scientific model on which they draw.

The first supposes that the object contains the sensuously experienced qualities by which it is encountered. In the case of the first flying saucer sightings, descriptions emerged of colour, material appearance and shape, together with judgements of distance, number and behaviour, leading to questions of provenance, design and intention (exhibited in elusiveness and the ability to anticipate human responses), and to speculations about powers of telepathy, clairvoyance and healing. All these could be called products of an animist frame of reference, with primary experience taken to contain its own explanation. Bachelard, from whom this classification derives,[2] labels this style 'pre-philosophical', but it nevertheless lies at the roots of realism and empiricism, for the experienced qualities are attributed significance.

The second accompanies the first and is an empirical approach, with the aim of precise determination and an emphasis on measurement and the use of instruments. Here we find calibration and recording; this style includes inventing equipment and techniques to grasp better the qualities displayed, and the concepts employed are held to be the 'clear, simple and infallible substitute for primary experience' (Bachelard 2008: 26). The use of the instrument allows thought about a stable and given world. In this approach, it is as if the instrument were independent of theory; we might say that technology employed thus has no need of science: the instrument has an obvious use and a sense of 'rightness'. Although this is not in fact true for modern scientific instruments, where theory precedes the instrument and is realized in it, and the relation between the instrument's mechanism and what it shows is not obvious, nevertheless, in practical

---

[2] See the first chapter of Bachelard's essay, *La philosophie du non* (Bachelard 1940).

terms radar has been used as if it were a pre-theoretical instrument, straightforwardly translating an experienced object in a realist fashion, so that to detect the presence of an object, track its trajectory and measure its speed is to capture the object in thought. The technical fixes initiated by the Air Force's Project Blue Book in the early 1950s in particular have the air of empiricist attempts to measure the phenomenon, where the body is held to contain its own principles. And the same is true of various attempts to measure levels of radiation associated with encounters. These realist forms of procedure, habits of thought and styles of explanation remain active within the milieu of an advanced science. This empiricist bias may appear particularly in the pragmatic approach associated with the engineer and the intelligence operative.

The third style of explanation begins to look for generalities, rules that can explain the regularities of events, so that certain principles can in combination generate the variety of phenomena encountered. This is the period of Ruppelt's consultants, Menzel's scepticism, and the continuing conflict between Menzel and his followers and the more scientific of Keyhoe's successors such as Macdonald (see Ruppelt 2011; Menzel 1953; Keyhoe 1950). The concept used is then part of a body of ideas and no longer a primitive element of immediate, direct experience. 'Scientific' thought is often held to have emerged in this moment when we move from a realist view of the world to a dynamic understanding of the grounds which permit the being realism describes. The procedures of scientific thought are at one remove from empiricism, and it becomes clear that, as we have suggested in the case of radar 'sightings', radar registrations do not simply measure the passage of flying objects but require further interpretation, so that correlation with other events – such as a visual sighting – take on a different and more indirect significance. One can then 'save' appearances by such a detour.

Following Bachelard's account, to preserve realism one has to pass from a realism of things to a realism of laws (Bachelard 2008: 29) and to the division of reality into two orders, with increasing complexity of levels and forms in the second, rule-governed level informing the world of experience. These rationalist concerns culminated in the ambition of positivism in the 1880s to subsume and organize all knowledge within the horizon of a single set of universal laws. Such concerns underlie a good deal of the attention paid to flying saucers once realist accounts failed to produce any unambiguous evidence, allowing theories that invoke even sociological or psychological causes to explain the reports of sightings as fictions or errors; these accounts often bring in earlier literatures, both of sightings in the late nineteenth century and folklore accounts.

Despite the still-dominant common-sense understanding of scientific knowledge, the rationalist account of reality as a law-governed world of empirical objects is not the last word, and two further approaches emerged in the first third of the twentieth century. The fourth style of explanation is a function of public understanding of the Theory of Relativity, which Bachelard sees as both the opening up of the rationalist model and as its completion. In the Newtonian account, space, time and mass stand as basic presuppositions, fundamental elements serving as the basis of any system of measurement and not in themselves open to further analysis. However, it became clear that mass has an internal structure (as opposed to external relations with force and acceleration); that rather than existing as a simple element, absolute in time and space and the basis for a system of absolute units, it is discovered to be a function of velocity, so that the mass of an object is relative to the object's displacement. In a like fashion, the determination of space and time becomes entangled, giving the emergent genre of science fiction its dominant theme of time travel (cf. Wittenberg 2013).

In short, the rational principles at stake come into question because it becomes clear they cannot be seen as independent variables but as interacting and affecting one another. There is a shift in perception: the concept – of mass, for example – can still operate as a simple notion for various applications – *a priori* rational constructions where approximation may serve – but is also available for increasingly plural, complex uses in others, depending on the degree of accuracy required for the work in hand.

This shift made rationalism no longer the baseline of ordered thought but, as Bachelard puts it, 'functional, diverse and lively' (Bachelard 2008: 32). And the realist, he notes, having already had to concede a duality between things and laws, now must recognize a more complex account of laws, with orders of scale and degrees of approximation. But the fundamental challenge to realism comes from the loss of any simple notion of 'the given'. Realism is based on a notion of dealing with a given object, yet advances in a science depend on overturning this point of view, simultaneously revising the object, detecting its internal structure, and reconstructing the nature of the knowledge gained, in this way changing the constitution of the science. We move from a world where both knowledge and what is known are stable and independent of one another to one where both are mutable and interdependent. For, as Bachelard insists, 'completed rationalism' is the result of thought and of the expression of thought, leading to the reform and reorganization of categories. Intellectual or mental powers take on quasi-causal properties.

Regarding the history of flying saucer investigations, in the early period (1947–1953), when security concerns were uppermost, realism was the appropriate attitude, with the application of rationalist methods. This perspective allowed the technical fixes tried out, the realist correspondences proposed between radar and visual sightings, and the business of scientists explaining away reports as mistakes made concerning natural objects. That last practice continued up to the Condon Report in 1968 and continues in a line of sceptical inquirers whose appeal to rationalism, however, fails to carry widespread conviction.

Even in the early period, there were hints of shifting realities and changing apprehensions, including revisions of the past. The implications of completed rationalism, that categories alter, that simple facts and laws are not a sufficient apparatus to grasp all phenomena, and that investigator and object of investigation may affect one another, were embraced and given form with respect to flying saucers from the 1960s onward: these help explain the successor forms of aliens and extra-terrestrial intelligence, engaging with human concerns from near at hand, in the case of abductions, and in images of elsewhere, in the case of potential communications from other planets. These concerns appear particularly when the craft display mind-like properties, as if they anticipated and understood the human responses to their presence, coming and going in a fashion that recalls the behaviour of goblins. Keel's work on the crafts' understanding of human political boundaries, calendars and times also comes under this heading (Keel 2013). And the idea that alien intelligence includes both their advanced physical scientific knowledge and their extraordinary mental powers (borrowed from the theosophists) fits well with this perspective.

Bachelard also identified a fifth approach, that of 'dialectical rationalism'. He draws attention to the implications of Dirac's theoretical discovery of two possible masses for a single electron, one corresponding to earlier philosophies, the other negative. Negative mass is inconceivable in both the perspective of realism and of rationalism, Newtonian or completed. So, while half of Dirac's discovery continues classical and relativist mechanics, the other half diverges on a fundamental notion. Bachelard depicts this theory as a further extension of the power of reason, the zone where the 'new scientific mind' reflects on thought's achievements. The theory has its own demands, seeking the realization of new concepts without any root in common reality (Bachelard 2008: 36). Although negative mass is an unknown, speaking in terms of phenomena, it is a precise unknown, neither vague nor irrational. Further, when features are confirmed in experimental results (as in the discovery of the positron), it offers an instance of nature being forced to recognize a product of the mind.

In his 1940 essay, Bachelard speculated whether we might be able to relate negative and positive mass to problems of disappearing and appearing, dematerialization and creation, and negative and positive energy (Bachelard 2008: 38). He did so to indicate the potential of the instructed mind to conjure realities through its powers of mathematizing, complexifying and multiplying entities. These possibilities clearly lend themselves to supporting occult or metaphysical claims. Anybody paying attention to the scientific developments of the period would have grounds for believing that the contemporary period supported claims, arising in the last third of the nineteenth century, of the power of mind over matter and of thought over nature (cf. Turner 1974). The notion that representatives of civilizations with more advanced technologies than ours could hover and accelerate effortlessly, materialize and disappear at will, and read humans' minds and anticipate their actions, all found their support, legitimately or otherwise, in contemporary physics. Last, therefore, we also find explanations which take account of the creative powers of human intelligence, exploring the dependence of the visitors on human response and participation, as if our minds too have the power to create realities. This possibility appears in the contactee Adamski but is writ large in some of the writings on abductions and is anticipated by Keel.

A structure to the spectrum of positions

In short, the various accounts with which we have been concerned contain a range of coherent presuppositions, and these all find support from scientific styles of explanation available in the period. Or, to put it the other way round, these scientific proposals as to the nature of the real were taken over and put to work in a series of improvisations. All were also explored by contemporary science fiction writers.[3] Bachelard, as we have seen, gives the styles names: animism, empiricism, rationalism, completed rationalism, and dialectical rationalism. The question now is whether there is an underlying structure to this series of improvisations, a second layer to these shared resources.

In the case of the people concerned in making and receiving reports of flying saucers, this structure is to hand and is not reflected upon; it is found in the series of unproblematic descriptions which allow a variety of practical engagements, the exploitation of scientific discoveries for human moral ends. But we need a way of conceptualizing the series so as to bring out a deeper structure, for it contains broader styles of thought that permit different human strategies or ways of being in the world. Bachelard offers us a way of doing this by translating the scheme in terms of a spectrum constructed between realist approaches and more imaginative employments of thought.

His broad concern was with the unprecedented nature of scientific discoveries in the first forty years of the twentieth century, and this clearly puts him in the same area as our project; novelties such as the appearance of flying saucers cannot be rejected on *a priori* grounds, for we have grown accustomed to advances which radically revise our understanding of the

---

[3] And one can play the game of matching theory to story. James Blish is particularly acute on the discovery of negative matter and its implications; see his *Galactic Cluster* (Blish 1959), which contains two stories in which negative mass and energy are put to work, first to allow a form of instantaneous communication at any distance, and then to power a spaceship drive. Blish also investigates the possibility that paranormal effects might be expected to accompany these moments of stepping outside the conventional real.

nature of reality and transform our technical and ethical possibilities. Flying saucers, it was claimed, are simply the advanced notice of yet further such discoveries. Moreover, Bachelard focussed on the technical production of new scientific phenomena rather than any uncovering of the secrets of the natural world; his interest centred on the human construction of new scientific effects, and this concern with technology provides further common ground.

He called this production a 'phenomenotechnics' – the technique of creating new phenomena – or 'applied rationalism'. From our point of view, the significance of this focus on the human production of new knowledge is twofold. On the one hand, there will be progress in understanding in a specific area of research as hypotheses or models are proposed, explored, tested and modified or discarded; earlier theory, now recast as error, is a crucial aspect of scientific development. On the other hand, existing generalizations, models now drawn from common sense and to hand for the interpretation of new phenomena, must be identified and largely set aside in this process of discernment. Both these aspects of scientific knowledge arise from the technical nature of research: one cannot make sense of new knowledge by recourse to existing mental plans and understandings because the production of scientific knowledge lies elsewhere. The new therefore takes priority, rather than being fitted to the existing proformas: progress is recursive, consisting in the repeated correction of previously held accounts, together with the incorporation of discarded hypotheses as the 'struck-out' candidates, which may be redeployed in unexpected ways as the explanatory framework develops and changes. In this fashion, 'epistemological obstacles' are incorporated in the history of the science in question, and error plays a continuing part in the progress of understanding. This approach gives us a frame for making sense of the history of flying saucers which, as we have seen, are interpreted by borrowing from models – 'struck-out candidates' – which were born in moments of scientific progress, but which had become common-sense ideas as the public used these advances to think with, to make sense and to offer discriminations.[4]

4   For accounts of Bachelard's methods, see the essays in Canguilhem (1970) and Rheinberger (2010).

Bachelard's work falls into two periods, with some early case studies of scientific discoveries followed by a series of epistemological writings in the 1940s and early 1950s, in the latter instance advancing some more general concepts including that of a 'philosophical spectrum'. The notion of an obstacle appeared in Bachelard (1938) and that of a scheme of scientific concepts was introduced in 1940; the idea of a philosophical spectrum appeared in 1949. It represents a shift in emphasis from the variety of scientific models to a coherent scheme employed in the sphere of argument and common sense. The philosophical positions identified served as representations that might act equally as stimulus or as obstacle in the individual scientific understandings being constructed in each case study. In short, I have taken the concept of a scheme of scientific models to offer a description of the range of kinds of representation used to grasp the emerging forms of flying saucers, a minor story in the margins of the experimental sciences of the period in question. The question now is whether a broader structure underlies the putting to work of these varieties of thought.

Two poles

We are working from the other side to Bachelard's main scientific interests, for we are concerned largely with the 'obstacles' from which scientific discoveries, which are real and not pre-ordained, have to distinguish themselves.[5] Yet the life of these obstacles is multiple; on the one hand, they may mix and interact with each other and, on the other, they play many roles, sometimes obstructing the development of understanding, sometimes cooperating with advances in knowledge, and even, in their turn, making new discoveries possible or generating something on their own behalf. These are images, representations taken from scientific thought, which continue to play their part in social life, in both formal and informal institutions.

---

5 Bachelard also wrote a series of literary studies towards the end of his career, exploring the creative aspects of these common-sense images (e.g. Bachelard 1958).

We can say two things about these images. First, although the models considered as hypotheses may appear in some sort of order as scientific models are tried and discarded in serial revisions, the positions as avatars, as representations, do not unfold in any linear fashion; they are all available in principle simultaneously, although, in practice, some positions predominate over others in a given period. And second, although there is no sense of progress as such, as in the replacement of hypotheses, there is a sense in which we return to the same ground in different representations but with a different perspective, asking different questions and seeing different things.

In his later account, *Le rationalisme appliqué* (Bachelard 1949), Bachelard offers a broad framework which helps refine our grasp of the possible descriptions. In it, the common forms of representation can be arranged in a spectrum, running from a realist to an idealist pole, which may be glossed as expressing the rival explanatory claims that the basis of intelligibility lies in material objects, on the one hand, and in mental powers, on the other. In the case of flying saucers, we begin with naïve claims of a realist kind, that the objects are real and are either machines, of a provenance to be determined by elimination – a US secret weapon, a Russian secret weapon or decoy, interplanetary in origin – or natural phenomena – planets, clouds, reflections of earthbound moving objects, flocks of birds – which have been mistaken for machines. The realist half of the spectrum includes empiricist and positivist claims, the belief, first, that the problem can be resolved by the examination of cases – the gathering of data and a series of technical fixes – and second, that the instances will turn out to be the expression of universal, unchanging natural principles. Put together, these two forms imply that, once we have examined and understood the cases, we will be able to classify the new objects as an expression of what is already known, at least in part: they will be new instances of known phenomena. They circumscribe the method of residues.

If these representations prove unsatisfactory, we can turn to explanations which seek to understand the phenomena in terms of appearances and their underlying causes, which invoke social and mental factors, looking to deceptions and delusions – hoaxes or treachery – or to 'mental instability' on either a collective or an individual basis – 'mass hysteria' or 'self-hypnosis' – or simply to fictions, either acknowledged or taken for real. Beginning from the centre of the spectrum, we move through formalism, a psychologized form of positivism, to conventionalism, taken as collective forms of error, and then to the idealist pole. In this optic, if the phenomena are not real, they must be lies or dreams, mistakes or stories.

Here we glimpse the problem that, although talk of a spectrum with its two poles will serve us well, it is not altogether satisfactory. As we shall see in the next chapter, the second pole on the scale of forms has its own activity and properties and is not simply a catalogue of attempts to cover over insufficiencies in the realist position. In this regard, Bachelard's earlier project of making a philosophical 'profile' of the concept of mass, with dialectical rationalism as the far point of the series, contains a better clue; we remain on the same ground but discover new characteristics, arrangements and potentials. There is more to the second pole than talk of two equivalent but incompatible positions allows.

Put together, the forms of representation in Bachelard's scheme lie in a loose spectrum. These are the kinds of 'explanation' that actors of any stripe reach for when confronted with these novel forms of life that are experienced in the various disturbances described and given shape in reports of sightings. Yet these representations neither can be detached from the event, for registration forms part of the simultaneity of the appearance, nor can they be taken to explain the phenomenon making its appearance. They may rather be thought of as a series of exercises in mapping the phenomena, mappings which miss a good deal of what is going on.

What is being missed? In brief, these phenomena show features of both poles; they display characteristics both of material objects and of mental powers. They are machines which show intentional behaviour, technologies which anticipate human reactions and, indeed, display signs of collective action. At the same time, they are clearly a function of a given stage of human history, objects that behave like cinematic images, relating to scientific and technological advances, and bound up with military and industrial concerns. Flying saucers are neither fully autonomous, that is, 'natural' objects, nor simply a projection of human preoccupations. They offer a mix of the positions on the spectrum.

In this regard, we might think of them as 'images' in the sense Bergson gives the term. Bergson suggests that images have 'an existence ... halfway between the "thing" and the "representation"' and that it is 'a mistake to reduce matter to the perception which we have of it, a mistake also to make of it a thing able to produce in us perceptions' (Bergson 2016: 9). Our concern is with images in this sense, and we shall consider the kinds to be met with in our investigations of reports in more detail in the next chapter.

CHAPTER 2

Sightings and reports

We have identified a range of contemporary ways of 'making sense', ways of ordering impressions and imparting order to the world through sets of presuppositions which allow understanding and ends-oriented behaviour. Forms of perception and action are imposed that allow both understanding of and intervention in the world. Our purpose now is to explore the characteristics of these forms in more depth, characteristics which as we have seen come in two broad kinds, those oriented towards practical action and those turned towards contemplation or observation. Perhaps the most important thing to say is that one does not observe in order to act; they are different kinds, one focussed on action, the other on description. And the second important thing to say is that the accounts proposed by realism and idealism, to give the broad kinds names, are useful guides but are not true in any abstract or absolute sense; they are rather means which human actors adopt under different circumstances in order to fulfil their purposes, purposes which of course may change according to altered circumstances and recourse to a different metaphysical scheme.

I want to make two proposals as to how we think about these schemes. The first is that human activities will by and large be pragmatic – ends-oriented and consisting largely in action – until the surrounding apparatus for making sense fails. Under a variety of circumstances, the taken-for-granted presuppositions that allow action to proceed without reflection cease to work. In particular, at certain points, units of measurement become inoperative, and the actors therefore lack appropriate second-order categories against which to calibrate their judgements and aims. Under these circumstances, which may be temporary and local, but which are recurrent, action ceases to be the means for making sense; it loses its authority and naturalness, and the actors have to turn to another kind of practice, that of observation and description, seeking to understand the changed nature of the world with which they are confronted. Under these altered conditions, the presuppositions allowing the first kind of making sense will emerge into view, as will the local circumstances promoting the crisis. At the same time, many of the basic categories by which we normally make sense in and of the world will be revealed to be both more arbitrary and less secure than we had supposed, and we glimpse the inherent complexity even of such basic notions as identity, opposition and non-contradiction, causality, and space and time.

In short, humans are practical creatures until the ground rules cease to work in some regard and we are brought to reflect. Plato says something similar in *The Republic*, concerning our perceptions: 'I can point to some of these which do not provoke thought to reflect upon them, because we are satisfied with the judgement of the senses. But in other cases, perception seems to yield no trustworthy result, and reflection is instantly demanded' (Plato VII, 522). However, although the contrast is an old one, it takes on new form in the modern period.

My second proposal is that the two schemes with which we are concerned, images caught up in action, on the one hand, and those demanding reflection, observation and description, on the other, find corresponding forms in film. If flying saucer sightings are like action films in the beginning, at a certain point, their style undergoes an inflection; abductions in particular are more like avant-garde films, concerned with repetitions, alternative paths, the significance of small events and gestures. It is worth asking why this might be so.

The spectrum we have identified borrows its forms from natural scientific thinking; it is in one regard a survey of ways of understanding the world – the real – created in collaboration with the modern sciences and technology. Our contemporary understanding of the nature of reality relies in large part on the discoveries of the sciences and the technologies that correspond to them. Among these discoveries, the world is conceived of in terms of wavelengths and particles (rather than as solids and their states), and the corresponding technologies include the possibility of 'total' recording of sound and light waves, embodied in the invention in the 1880s of the gramophone and film. This is to follow Kittler's thesis (Kittler 1999). And film came rapidly to incorporate the recording of both light and sound (or, in our terms, sightings and reports).

Film is interesting in such a context because, on the one hand, it was made possible by a conception of the world in terms of wavelengths and particles and, on the other, it sought to convey the experience of living in such a world; it did not abandon the world of solids and states but, at the same time, it sought to explore the impasses and contradictions such a world contained, its limits and alternatives. In this fashion, it also portrays the variety of time-relations possible and, in so doing, the range of alternative presuppositions available. For if we conceive of the material world primarily in terms of communication, of the recording, storage and transmission of wavelengths, what is the case and how we know it are recast. And so is the portrayal of the social and ethical condition, which may be understood in terms of rhetoric and persuasion – establishing character, sharing emotion, creating common grounds of demonstration.

A range of philosophers in the first part of the twentieth century sought to produce a metaphysics adequate to the modern sciences, 'a metaphysics in which the concept of multiplicity replaces that of substance, event replaces essence and virtuality replaces possibility' (to cite Smith and Protevi 2014). Bergson and Bachelard were among these philosophers, as was Whitehead (who is outside my scope). Also, later, Gilles Deleuze, who used a close reading of Bergson to explore the nature of cinema, conceived as capturing aspects of the world which were invented by modern technologies, particularly of communication, and detailing the shifts in social life and human experience which accompany these aspects (Deleuze 2001, 2005). For these reasons, his work is extraordinarily useful for exploring the different schemes we have identified, although my primary focus is not on film but on the film-like aspects of thought about images of life elsewhere. Analogies drawn from cinema will serve as some sort of key to the always-partial processes of making sense in and of such a world.[1]

---

1 Deleuze's two books shape what I have to say in the remainder of this chapter. While I cite him repeatedly, this is not meant to be an exposition of Deleuze's theories of the cinema, which are far more sophisticated than this broad description

We will begin by considering images oriented to practical action, the anomalies that emerge and the kinds of characters we find in these images, and the limits they point to in the realist scheme.

I. A realist narrative

If we are using cinema as a prompt to think about the presuppositions that appear in the various reports of sightings, Adamski's narrative in his first book (Leslie and Adamski 1953) offers a clear place to start. He sets up a situation which includes the narrator in a wider setting of mysterious events, events which hint at the possibility of an encounter, he then focusses on the moment of meeting in an accelerated passage, which comprises the action in the story, and finally he leaves us with a thoroughly altered understanding of our situation and its potential. He uses binary relations to move the story along: a series of confrontations between enquirers and sceptics, the open-minded seekers and men-in-the-know, men-in-the know and obscure opponents, the one more local and the other more metropolitan, and, repeating the last opposition on a wider scale, humans and visitors. And we pass rhythmically between the parties, building up an accelerating rhythm. In the framing or the build-up, a series of nested flashbacks are also given which elaborate the initial situation, depicting timely signs to be read which form the education both of the narrator and the reader. There is a temporal structure to this work of deciphering portents, of recovering the past and adjusting earlier intuitions, which leads to the discovery both of the reality of interplanetary visitors and of the complex politics being played by the security forces in response to these appearances.

When we come to the moment of meeting, we find the wider issues focussed within the single figure of the enquirer and we learn his emotional

---

allows. I have used his thinking as inspiration for my own; he, of course, gave no consideration to the kind of topics I have put his ideas to.

responses. In this fashion, we swap between the large scale and the small, turning to parts that exemplify wholes, so that the human readers learn simultaneously about a single person's experience and reactions and the potential future of the human race, for good or evil. And although this wider background story fades from sight when we come to the encounter, with its detail of garments, machines and agenda of topics for discussion, it comes back into view in the aftermath, for we are left with the demand that collectively we follow a different course of action in response to the reality disclosed: a different human politics and far greater dependence on the wisdom and good-will of the visitors. This is a typical action story of the period: the narrative has a clear, progressive structure, accumulating first hints and then evidence of a threat and then the possibility of redemption, each stage preparing for the next, first clarifying mystery and menace but then containing that menace in the accelerating detail of successive contacts and the teaching received from the Space Masters. The alternatives – of crisis or redemption – are left open before the reader.

In short, while we are given little significant material on emotional involvement or character development, we instead have an action schema: an initial situation leading seamlessly to a moment of decisive action which, in turn, results in an altered situation. And the protagonist, as our representative, copes with every crisis and twist, revealing the material the story has given him.

Adamski's later books repeat the same structure but with less impact. Because they focus on the teaching imparted during the encounters, we learn more about how the space brothers understand our present earthly situation and their calling to us to mend our ways now that the true situation has been disclosed (although effectively we learn nothing we did not already know), but, as a consequence, the narrative lacks the drama and confrontations of the first meeting.

It is worth adding that there is a common enough variant to this pattern of 'situation-action-changed situation', which is to begin with an action, then explore the situation which results from that action (sometimes with the help of retrospective recollection), before concluding with a second action which restores the status quo or develops the situation in, usually, a hopeful direction. The reports we have of Close Encounters tend to follow this second pattern, where we start with a sighting and explore the ramifications, opening onto an account of changed lives. Here, there may be more evidence of character development.

We might notice in passing that, in science fiction stories and films, the main confrontations are usually fought out between humans, between enquirers and sceptics, then military misunderstandings of or reticence over ufologists' insights, sometimes (in a spaceship or on a planet) rivalries between military men or scientists. The appearance of aliens usually serves to reconcile these contests; their role is rather minor in this regard, and they usually serve as an ally rather than an opponent of the human protagonist. A further observation: the appearance of aliens also introduces an element of time travelling, not simply to overcome the enormous distances in space, but to explain the possibility of sympathy and communication between kinds. We glimpse our future selves in these men or creatures returning to our time. This factor does not, I think, seriously undermine the model of time at work, but it introduces some complexity. Wittenberg (2013) sketches the dilemmas but also notes the generally conservative nature of the solutions adopted.

These are what we have called realist accounts; they contain animist elements – objects which are explained by their qualities – and they encourage empiricist investigations. The question now is, what are the ground rules that allow both these realist narrative patterns to work? The narrative presupposes, first, a coherent and rule-governed world where inference and deduction are possible, where ambiguities of interpretation are few and readily resolvable, and where there is an economy of effort and result, which are held to be proportionate. All this is held within a horizon against which everything makes sense. And second, corresponding to this world condition, there is an internal consciousness which allows the narrator-cum-actor to grasp the situation and to take decisive action on that basis, action that will contribute meaningfully to the world that has been grasped and even to help make the new situation that results. The actor is, as it were, part of the ordered and in theory transparent world condition. In short, action makes sense, both in the world and of the world; there is a coherent cosmic horizon and a coherent internal person silhouetted against it. There is little here of contingency, plurality of viewpoint, blindness of actors or unintended consequences; all these are possible but, in the end, will be resolved and seen for what they are: confusions or errors.

Bergson (2016) characterizes such an account as depending in the actor on a 'sensory-motor' schema, by which perception is translated into action through the intermediary of affective response. In this fashion, there is necessarily a delay, an interval between the reception of a given stimulus and the physical response to it, a moment of registration, interpretation and feeling or affect. This interval might be called the present moment.

Deleuze notes that, in this understanding of the world and our place in it, time is imagined in two ways and both are dependent on the primacy granted action or movement. On the one hand, time consists in an empirical succession of present moments, running from moments which were present but now are past towards future moments, each a present to come. On the other hand, time operates at a second level, that of the measure or calibration of the narrative of actions and their moments, and that in this second regard it has two aspects: it is the minimum interval between movements, and it is the sum total of movement in the universe. These are the limits, internal and external, of the scales at which the model works, both operating within the logic of coherent action.

Anomalies

Adamski, then, perhaps surprisingly, works with a consistent metaphysics, offering a realist grasp on the world and its planetary environment. His assumptions were widely shared, including by the various reports made of Close Encounters, allowing both the gathering of evidence – photos, taking moving film, making castes and collecting other traces, recording levels of radioactivity – and efforts to revise known scientific laws to explain such phenomena as the speed of movement of craft, the source of their energy, their appearances and disappearances both in sight and on radar tracking, the stresses the acceleration and manoeuvrability of the craft must exert on the bodies within, and so forth. A correlate to such realist accounts is the subordinate place granted to mental effects, acts of imagination, fictions, dreams and memories; such virtual effects, as imaginary objects, must be based on actual things (cf. Crane 2013). Adamski was attacked by his critics, indeed, for mistaking such imaginary objects for reality.

Yet we could look at matters in another light. The anomalies which emerge may be construed as threatening the coherence of the realist schema and do so mainly by raising puzzles about the reliable nature of the measurements and calibration employed and about the nature of time. Anomalies appear particularly in 'psychical' phenomena – the various mental capacities attributed to the visitors. These capacities appear in their ability to monitor human thought processes and behaviour, their powers of hypnotism, suggestion and mental control, their communicating telepathically with one another and with chosen human subjects, shown when they select and contact such individuals or draw them to a meeting, and, on another scale, by their foresight and, indeed, their practical omniscience about human affairs and life on other planets, their qualities as future men, returning to monitor and educate the present human race and, at the highest level, their direct communication with the Cosmic Mind. And we ought to note, too, the corresponding development of psychical gifts in the human subjects selected for communication, as they gain telepathic reception and even the power of summoning their masters to a meeting, the ability to recognize visitors in their human disguise, and the sense of vocation and seizing the time that marks sharing with the Cosmic Spirit.

All these signs tend to disturb the empirical succession of moments and undermine the notion of the interval that underwrites the sequence of actions and gives access to the rhythms and patterns ordering the cosmic totality. They do this because they suggest the reversal of the subordination of mental features to action; they propose the intrusion of the virtual – imagination, memory, dreams – into the actual world of things, facts, movements and acts. In this fashion, psychical phenomena signal a *crisis* in the realist understanding of the world as a place best made sense of in terms of pragmatic action, consisting primarily in sensory perception and physical response. It is the nature of this interaction between virtual and actual that concerns us, signalled by the prominence of psychical phenomena; the phenomena are not important of themselves.

Where do these anomalies emerge? Let us return to the narrative presuppositions of realism – the coherent universe confronted by a self-conscious actor. By self-conscious, we mean the actor's internal voice, speaking to himself (and to us) as he monitors the world, classifies the puzzles it raises and seeks their resolution, always acting through confrontation with others and so expressing that consciousness through action. This narrative has to take the form of a succession of moments, for only in this fashion can the actor grasp movement, that is, change in the world. Yet, by grasping it in this fashion, the true nature of movement is lost sight of, for we cannot grasp the emergence of new things directly by a notion of succession, nor, by imposing such an idea of sequence, can we glimpse the possibility that the categories by which such novelty is apprehended also change. In short, succession is a poor form for grasping the nature of 'events' – which may also be called 'emergence', or a 'singularity', or a 'phase change' – for the conditions allowing memory to work change at the same time as the thing to be understood shifts in nature, together with the part it plays in the whole, which in turn is restructured. Indeed, under these conditions where memory, understanding and aim (or desire) all mutate, the notion of personal identity with a consistent internal voice becomes difficult to sustain.

Nevertheless, there are different ways of working with succession within the horizon of realist narratives and we meet these different ways in the types of character or roles that appear in reports of encounters. There are three distinct types, each with its own timeline, which will be our concern for the remainder of this section.[2]

First character

The first role is associated with the claim to make authoritative judgements about the reported phenomena. It is embodied in a person such as a well-respected scientist or a military officer, but the same authority

---

2   These recall features of the three forms of social logic discussed in the fourth essay, *UFO Reports*.

was also sought by the investigators authorized by the various organizations, networks, committees, centres and so forth that coordinated research into flying saucer sightings, and claimed too by the rival sceptical groups seeking to debunk their findings. These actors all work with a linear timeline, assuming a narrative of successive episodes and places. The principals who move along this line have individuality, achievements and reputation; we know who they are. We might say they have a destiny. In Adamski's story, these are the scientists, the military men, the engineers, the men in the know. They have the upper hand in the organizing narrative, even if this is sometimes disputed. Along this line, the various groups concerned are organized hierarchically, so that some other players have lesser parts and provide the major players with their material; these are the people who bring reports, whose testimony is to be evaluated, or intermediaries like the police or neighbours. In this organization, structure is everything. High-ranking officers based at a distance may hold different views from their field operatives, but they stand together in opposition in terms of authority to the witnesses and their supporters who, again, may have differences among themselves as to what has taken place. Whatever an individual's commitments, the position of men with authority and a narrative of succession trumps the experience of witnesses every time, organizes the dealings between the parties and determines the outcome of any investigation which always ends in the impossibility of making any decisive judgement; it is impossible that either party's mind will be changed. Motivation and character are curiously unimportant in these confrontations; actors in any part of this narrative may hold a range of private opinions, sympathies or even agendas, they may be thoroughly honest, or flawed, but what matters is who they are with relation to the organizing narrative: each plays their part according to their situation, in relation to the regular line of a sequence of presents. Deleuze calls this form a segmentary line.

A second kind of existence

There is also a second kind of relation to the temporal sequence of events, which is found in the experience of those making reports; these experiences are far less unified, in fact and in aspiration. If the first kind has a certain solid, fixed quality, the second is more fluid; there is less structure to the episodes they live through, which rather constitute a series of transformations. The actors are vulnerable and are carried to curious fates; they are mobile both in person and status and, because more mobile, they can participate in exchanges. They take on qualities from the objects that fascinate them; they have meetings with strangers and alter their way of life; they leave partners and friends and assort with others; sometimes they gain powers of intuition and mental communication. Their desires change; they become different people, and, because of this mutability, they lack the defining character of the first kind of actor. As they undergo a series of transformations, they do not lend themselves to the comparisons between orders that structure the first kind of relation; rather, we find slippage between different stages along the series and, at the same time, from the first perspective, a lack of definition: witnesses are interchangeable and, by the same token, egalitarian rather than hierarchically ordered. There is then a different, second kind of line in relation to the sequence of time, a line which Deleuze calls one of 'becoming', meaning this kind of transformation through engagement with another and taking on new properties because of that engagement; in short, a series of short-term affairs, of escapes from the power of the first kind of line.

It is worth remarking that these fates, despite their lack of structure and their fluidity, appear if left to themselves to be self-sustaining, and that when disaster intervenes, it does so because of engagement with the first kind of line. Either the actor tries to borrow some aspect of the first kind, such as appealing to the rule book or claiming an authority which cannot be sustained, or the more elusive, multiple form of life is captured, tamed and domesticated by the first kind. We could see the fate of many witnesses in these terms; they become encompassed by representatives, investigators and journalists, and also trapped by techniques: the introduction of the Geiger counter, the investigation of documents and their substitution, the threat of hypnotic regression on television, the lie detector tests; in the end, they become turned into exhibits.

The narrative form which begins from an act or event is well-suited to this second kind of actor or role, for it starts out from a confrontation between parties and is narrowly focussed at the scale of the person. The first form, as we saw, begins at the larger scale; at the outset, we grasp the unity of the situation and the integration of its elements, then we sense the tension between parts which leads in due course to a confrontation or, rather, to a series of confrontations, struggles in which the protagonist first realizes what he has to do and finds his feet, and, after setbacks and with assistance, finally achieves his end. The second form reverses this pattern; we deduce the situation from the action, which instructs us in a smaller scale, a mode of behaviour, a fragment of a way of life. In this form, a slight initial difference – a small clue – may reveal a choice between two very different possibilities: is this a prank or truly a visitor from another planet? The sign or clue in the situation may indicate a vast off-stage presence. For this reason, the second form of narrative and kind of actor introduce thought; we have to make inferences, and this binds the reader (or viewer) into the action and allows the play of the imagination. The virtual is no longer secondary. The lack of definition of the protagonist and indeed of the situation are indicative of the problem realism confronts in these forms: we begin to lose sight of a real world made up of things that contain their own properties and facts that can be collected by empirical methods, a world arranged according to laws that can be discovered upon reflection. Instead, we move to a world where things do not readily join up and are not individually clear and distinct, each lacking an identity, no longer separated in space and time, closed to inspection and classification.

In practice, the first, 'larger' scheme contains the second, and once we have acknowledged the active possibility of thought, there are ways of moving between them, of passing from one scheme to the other. There are occasions when an ordinary object carries extraordinary significance, such as traces of a visit or a light in the sky behaving in an anomalous fashion; there can be small jarring scenes within the whole which anticipate the unfolding plot to come, as in glimpses of a visitor in an animal or a passing stranger; and there are those figures of thought shared by the protagonist and the reader alike (though often one is in advance of the other), when the penny drops and a new understanding of the world emerges, carrying its own sense of conviction and rightness of fit.

Realism is therefore under threat; in this second kind of actor and timeline we have already escaped from some of the constraints of the realist account. It is worth adding, as an aside, that realism is not realistic: we do not in everyday life find entire situations organized by connections and coherent forces, nor confrontations within them that focus these situations, leading to action and resolution. These are, at best, utterly exceptional states. Realism is only meant to be a narrative form. In life, we find multifactorial situations without clear overarching definitions, and actions take the form of small deeds rather than crises, often as attempts to gain a limited end directly, accompanied by unintended consequences or attendant factors which effectively defeat this aim. Instead of realist forms, we live by rhythms, habits and coping mechanisms, making connections and cutting ourselves off from other possibilities, and we deal with specific tasks using those habits and adding such skills and flair as we possess (see Jenkins 1994). Events take place at quite another level, largely in the collective redistribution of values and of the possibilities of interpretation and action. Realism is at most part of the shared resources by which we try to make sense of such a world, a narrative habit, one in which we attribute to ourselves (and others) capacities largely beyond our reach.

Encounters of a third kind

Last, there is a third figure in realist narratives, by which their presuppositions are further eroded, and, accompanying it, a third kind of line, supporting actors with neither a destiny nor a fate. These are, of course, the aliens or visitors, necessarily more elusive figures than those solid persons along the segmentary line or the fluid figures with their passing engagements marked by the continuous variation of desire. The visitors resemble gases, we might say, rather than solids or liquids, sharing some properties which may be outlined as follows.

First, their timeline begins before the narrative we are offered and continues after it, and it organizes everything significant that happens within the story. In Adamski's case – but he is in no way exceptional in this regard – the craft were there before our time; we trace earlier appearances in flashbacks, and then chart their approach in terms of distance and increase in frequency and boldness. We map their growing influence as they identify and call their contacts, placing interest in their subjects' minds, bringing them into new associations and practices of communication such as mediumship, and then leading them into the desert, before finally singling out the narrator for a face-to-face meeting. This is only the beginning of the story, but already everything is ordered and scripted by the visitors as they construct each event and respond to the situations they have conjured up. In this fashion, they permeate even the bodies of the human actors; they read their minds and influence their thoughts and actions.

Their mental powers are key. In physical regards, they appear confined: they are trapped within their craft, we presume, as they cover vast distances in space, although we glimpse their capacity for instant communication with their home planets, and their manoeuvrability once close to earth does not really compensate for this restriction. And when we glimpse them in the body, they lack much physical force or presence. In part, they rely on advanced technical equipment for monitoring human activities from a distance, but in practice all their strength lies elsewhere, in their mental powers which allow them to follow not only individual human thoughts but also the practices and intentions of governments and other organizations. They are in this sense ubiquitous.

Somewhat like Protestants, however, they rarely intervene above the level of the individual human conscience once contact has been made (though there are exceptions in fiction, such as the case of Arthur C. Clarke's Guardians, who work with governments and other human institutions and are not above using the threat of force; see Clarke 2010). By and large, they restrict themselves to engaging in dialogue with humans and seeking to persuade them, particularly to adopt more peaceful ways. Rather like children, we are first placed in a position we did not choose and then educated to use our free will. Nevertheless, they can also organize the mental faculties of human actors as well as play with appearances, and this raises a number of issues. We can never get to grasp their real motives, just as their advanced technical knowledge is far beyond our understanding. Because they can organize desire, they are effectively beyond good and evil; it is impossible to form any definitive judgement about them. As the abduction stories show, for this reason those who have been chosen tend to trust their abductors, seeking lasting relationships and meaning in these relationships despite every twist and turn in the story. It is only in the longer term that the relationship sometimes founders; towards the end of his life and after several quarrels and breaks, some of Adamski's followers formed views concerning factions within the visitors' ranks. Victims of abductions, reflecting on their experiences, have formed survivors' groups. And both Vallee and Keel's approaches in practice run aground around this issue; if the visitors (wherever they have come from) can organize memories, knowledge and feelings, human actors cannot recall the past or evaluate the present or make judgements with any accuracy or surety (see Keel 2014; Vallee 2014). In this fashion, despite their early offers of friendship and their seeming frailty, the limits of capacity and understanding that emerge, and even their dependence on the cooperation of the human race, the visitors are to be feared as well as loved, and their apparently benign intentions are balanced with fears of quasi-medical experimentation and breeding programmes.

These elusive qualities and the responses they elicit from the other actors point to the primary position of this third kind of line, which Deleuze calls the line of pure movement, which serves as the truth of the other two lines in the sense that it contains their meaning, their direction and desire. The power and rationality of the first kind of line are in this perspective illusory, as are the momentary, changing desires of the witnesses and their followers, for each can be organized by the imaginative mental force of this line without beginning or end. This organizing power is most clearly seen in the accounts of abduction where, despite their singularity, weakness and impotence, the visitors manipulate human memories and desires on a large scale, signalling their intentions with respect to the human race and this planet in ways which were only hinted at in earlier accounts.

A common man's philosophy

These three roles remain within the rules of a realist narrative in that we continue to deal with matter and its states, and the story unfolds in principle in a linear sequence with intentional movement as the focus. At the same time, the underlying 'engine' of perception leading to action, the sensory-motor scheme with its structuring interval comprising the delay between reception of the stimulus and physical response, becomes increasingly unreliable, and with it, the notion of a coherent universe made up of the sum of all such movements loses much of its sense. As a narrative form, realism can then be seen from two angles. On the one hand, it can be seen as a way of displaying the interactions and relations of the different roles and timelines, with the capacity to show in these interactions and relations matters that are due to neither thought nor action. On the other hand, it can be seen as displaying limits which call for another kind of narrative with other presuppositions.

We will come to the second angle in later sections. With regard to the first, as we have suggested, the focus on succession is a poor means to grasp the real nature of change in the sense of the emergence of new phenomena in the world, in part because it tries to map the new in already existing terms and so tends to miss the possibility of new categories by which to apprehend the novelty in question. Yet, by portraying specific interactions between these distinct kinds of actors, the narrative continually opens onto what cannot be seen elsewhere, changes in the whole or the set of elements, whereby alteration in some part becomes a symptom or sign of a shift in the relations making up the larger totality. Despite the literal idiom – the narrative of succession – employed by Adamski and by other reports of encounters, these accounts seek to portray a singularity, a moment of precipitation that marks a phase change in the whole, for example, a transfer in authority from those men in the know to those watching the skies, brokered by the third party, the visitors. We might say the whole mix has altered because one party has grasped something of the true nature of time as opposed to the accepted notion of succession.

These narratives then portray relations between parts as much as they do a succession of moments, and these relations have their own rhythm of movement and development. It is as if one put the players back into Saussure's analogy of a chess board: in a real game of chess, there are specific moves made which are game-changing, when the values of the pieces on the board alter decisively, moments which determine the story of the match (see Saussure 1974). It takes an experienced chess player to see them. In this regard, the sequence of moves points to another, real time, a history of events which passes at the level of the whole.

There are two ways of reading a story such as that offered by Adamski or the more partial accounts of Close Encounters. One is as a series of episodes, the other is as a sequence of connected transformations. In the latter case, we might look at moments of informal testing and independent confirmation, the appearance of evidence which not only hints at new possibilities but reveals something of the character and vocation of those being tested, and the development of social bonds and alliances with others on the same path, bonds which are formally tested in the initial encounter. The protagonist gains new powers from the encounter, distinguishing his fate (in the case of Adamski) from those allowed other companions, who are sometimes deprived of potential by their decisions, acts and refusals. The narrator retains his power of initiative and his mobility because of the relations he enjoys and the qualities he gains through his contact with the visitors, and these lead in turn to new encounters and new relations with followers, for good or ill. All these features are aspects of a single change. The narrator continually goes beyond his limits because of the relations he expresses, and through these relations participates in the life of different groups, using his engagements with representative members of the groups. While we speak of individuals, we are in fact dealing in the interactions of groups, of sets of people (and others), and it is through these sets that we glimpse the open nature of the whole, and the time of the events that organize the component elements is grasped.[3] This time is not sequential but a simultaneity, experienced through moments of crisis or judgement. This account gives content to the concept of an 'image', the ideal and material forms through which time constructs collective human lives.

3   Strieber (1987) is particularly acute on the collective nature of the visitor entity – the hive mind – encountered in a single representative – the mantis form.

A series of episodes along a single timeline then also carries with it another dimension, a history of transformations focussed in the narrator or witness, seen in his alliances and gaining new properties, his various achievements 'against the grain' – in some cases, advising the security apparatus, anticipating scientific and natural discoveries and world political events – and giving access to the real time of the whole, encompassing the fate of many other actors and the installation of a new normality, when new perceptions, practices and rules become routine.

In sum, there is a complex 'common man's philosophy' contained in these reports and their elaboration, a world conceived in terms not of bodies, qualities and actions but made up of interconnected processes, in perpetual movement, and ordered by impersonal events. It is not to suggest that this view is consciously developed, nor that it resolves all the problems it raises. In particular, the point of view of the narrator or observer is rarely integrated in any regard into the single account of a world of movement and process, nor is there a philosophy of life or living forms in general.[4] And Deleuze suggests that, because we grasp these processes in language using nouns, adjectives and verbs, we picture movement in the world as bodies in space directed by purposeful action, replacing the idea of the event by talk of purposes or ends, states, and subjects and objects. In this fashion, a 'normal' account of the world is preserved, and the world the modern sciences have revealed to us of a-centred movement, of continual change without points of anchorage or centres of reference, is lost sight of.[5]

---

4   Bergson claims the mark of living things is to create an interval between receiving the action of the surrounding world and offering a reaction, in this way introducing the possibility of registration and selection, reducing the input and producing difference. In this fashion, any living thing is a centre of indeterminacy in the mix, potentially constituting a subject.
5   See Deleuze (2001), chapters 9 and 10 for discussion of situation-action and its inverted form, chapter 4 for the sensory-motor scheme, and chapter 5 for the three kinds of roles.

II. Intermediate forms

Our next task is to give more detail on developments at the limits of the action model, looking at two intermediate forms of narrative, which we could call naturalism and modernism, on the way to formulating a second scheme in the following sections.

We could summarize the argument so far by saying that realist narratives contain the potential for their own overcoming because, as well as showing impressions that lead to actions, they also indirectly depict a third element, the evolving relations between parts which portray a single event, a shift in definitional as opposed to actual space. Nonetheless, a simultaneity of this kind is continually being covered over by practically oriented accounts which make sense by talk of purposes, states, subjects and objects, and assume a sequence to the moments that are produced by such talk. Under certain conditions, however, this kind of talk ceases to carry conviction, when the underlying means of measuring and calibrating the straightforward talk of what one sees, how one feels, and what to do about it, fail for some reason. Under these conditions, the underlying relations that are expressed in actions and perceptions may appear clearly in sight and demand another account of the world than that provided by realist presuppositions. As we shall see, in this second kind of scheme, not only events come to prominence, but also multiplicities stand in for single structures and series, and ideas and imagination come to play a part in the real world.

Deleuze suggests that, although the new scheme emerges primarily for reasons of internal logic, on grounds of the kind we have sketched and will continue to explore, there are also external conditions which correlate with and support this emergence. He points in particular to the post-War landscape and conditions of life there which did not readily support coherent narratives. It is a basic thesis of this whole account that the development of the relevant technologies and the wider history are closely connected, essentially as a history of warfare and its aftermath, and cannot be separated from the new images created and the human experiences which they explore, so that the external circumstances are incorporated in the evolving style of narrative.

I now will follow some intermediate steps in the history of flying saucer sightings within the broad pattern being explored, stations along the profile constructed in the previous chapter, leading (in the following sections) to a discussion of abductions and recovered memory within the perspective of a developed idealist scheme.

A first step

Keel's approach is the first systematic break with realism in the study of flying saucers (see Keel 2014).[6] How best can we characterize his achievement? He appeals to poltergeist-like entities which are mischievous, interact with modern technologies, particularly modern means of communication, react to human orderings – recognizing sites of strategic importance, political boundaries and times and days of the week – and also are able to anticipate and, to some extent, order human responses to their provocations. This is a form of literary naturalism – a genre born exactly contemporary with positivism – which describes humans in terms of animal and spirit properties, together with a morbid focus on death; Keel becomes increasingly pessimistic about the outcomes from these encounters in a human perspective.

If we imagine him in the same optic as Zola, he likewise offers us small episodes of ordinary lives, in which, however, we lose sight of the specific actors and their setting, for the protagonists do not explore the logic of that social world and its implications but instead encounter some fragmentary energetic form from a basic natural world. The typical elements – phone calls, mysterious summons, men in black – are stereotyped, as is the encounter as a whole: although the forces met with use words and give messages (though without significance) and understand some human boundaries and categories, they work by instinct, and we meet

---

6   Though there were always people like Meade Layne, George Williamson and others in Adamski's circle, not to mention Jack Parsons.

only fragments of entities, never wholes. The account then deals with a human world portrayed in realist terms, but in it the actors encounter a natural order in which the motive force is instinct rather than reason. And the actors are absorbed to the extent they cannot escape this natural order; they express these fragmentary forces so neither the forces nor the sense of the resulting human actions can be reconstituted and understood.

As with the earlier form of naturalism, we are given a diagnosis of the world in the grip of natural forces; American civilization, in this case, is conceived as a world where technical matters have taken over but to no purpose and without revealing any underlying order. Although the impulses experienced so far do not cause much disruption beyond the small-scale encounters described, they point to the possibility of greater disruption and, indeed, of degeneration and of loss of life.[7] This is where Clarke's tale of the Guardians comes in (Clarke 2010): we find the potential for perverse behaviours to take hold, for fragments torn from their settings to gain activity, for the energies released to pass from one setting to another, and for the whole story to end in death, even death of the human race.

Vallee appealed to goblins and fairy folk as model forms of the same kind. In both cases, the authors expand the form of life found in the second kind of role in realism, elaborating a human narrative based on short periods of interactions with non-human energies, of doomed affairs with the passions to the fore. Vallee particularly emphasized the sexual aspects of these hauntings, and both draw attention to parallels with the notion of psychological warfare developed in the period (Keel 1971; Vallee 1979; cf. Denzler 2001: 116–123). Nevertheless, at the same time both authors can appeal at an abstract level to the possibility of transcendence, of humankind cooperating in some notion of cosmic progress; again, Clarke spells this out in *Childhood's End*.

From the earliest days of reports, rationalist accounts supported realist rejections of sightings by appeal to psychological explanations, either invoking individual error and contagion or collective delusion, hysteria and so forth. In these two authors, we have a reversal, an acceptance of the

---

7 Keel also points to one larger scale event, the collapse of a road bridge into a river with loss of human lives. Fuller (1966a) mentions large scale electrical blackouts.

imaginary elements or, better, recognition that imaginary elements can impinge on and cause alteration within the sphere of the real. Jerome Clark (1998) and Méheust (2007) set out on this path and then both retreated to realism. In Keel and Vallee, we find a clear view of the insufficiencies of the realist position and the price to be paid in terms of loss of the actor's personality and intention, fragmentation of chains of reasoning, and the implication of both the observer and his proxy, the reader, in the picture.

The properties of the 'interval'

Abduction narratives share many similarities; they focus on small-scale encounters between humans and visitors, leading to a narrative that steps back sufficiently to indicate the elements of the setting that have been challenged or altered by the meeting, which in turn demand further action, often in the form of seeking to restore the informant's first state by offering therapy and healing, but also sometimes to prolong the engagement and develop the contact. As with Keel and Vallee, we find fragmentation of the narrative form with consequent loss of links between cause and effect and the forceful presence of imaginary or virtual kinds.

These narratives also contain a novel element, a detailed concern with the faculty of remembering. They focus on the reliability of memory and the possibility of recovering memories that have been lost or hidden, and then look for the causes of these forms of forgetting and their implications for any concept of human identity. By introducing hypnosis and the notion of recovered memory, we lose sight both of any idea of a coherent universe that can be make sense of in a broad fashion and of any possible unified human internal consciousness that can grasp the situation and take decisive action. We have nothing but short stretches of experience, even if repeating patterns can be discerned in them.

The crux is the sensory-motor schema that allows the matching-up of setting and consciousness with, at its heart, the delay or interval between stimulus and response. Once this schema collapses, the present moment disappears and with it the obviousness of the realist narrative, with its logic of coherent action. And with the evaporation of the present moment, we lose any possibility of a succession of moments, and time as a measure or calibration of such a succession ceases to mean much – the collapse of a second-order category, by which we make sense of life and its events – as does the notion of time as a horizon, the sum total of all such movement in the universe.

By introducing a focus on memory, abduction narratives necessarily concentrate on the internal, affective moment in the delay between perception and action in the schema that fails. They attempt to recover that lost time and, indeed, in doing so develop a whole philosophy of time. I will approach this question of a philosophy of time in two stages. First, in this section, we will look at the abduction event, rather than memory as such, to see the sharpening of the focus on affect in the early accounts and its contribution to the breakdown of realist histories. Second, in the following sections, we shall examine the elaboration of another account of memory in the later discussions of abduction, involving lives constructed around repeated encounters with their adjustments of memory, and even successions of such lives; here we find sketched, at least in part, a new account of human life in time. It is worth remarking, in this work, the difficulties of finding a consistent vocabulary to talk about different forms of time.

Nowhere-in-particular

The problem for the abductee is not simply that she (or he) cannot believe her eyes, but that she cannot remember what she has seen and what happened to her. This problem has a number of aspects. To begin with, the human response to what is seen is in part controlled by the visitors; Barney Hill, for instance, may have been summoned to the meeting, and certainly his fears were to a degree quieted, for he received reassurance. The actions he undertook were already not at one with the world he perceived. The ambiguity in the interval – how to respond? What feelings motivated the response? – is the product of the shift in the wider definitional space, for 'normal' parameters are not operating, and this wider shift is expressed in the individual's experience, in Barney's recurrent sense of fear and anxiety and Betty's sense of curiosity and even exuberance (see

Fuller 1966b). A shift at the collective level is linked with the emotions of an individual, and in this regard the individual is part of a far wider process.

In the 'moment' of encounter, then, we cannot be certain of the boundaries either of the person or of the situation, for the succession of moments is suspended and ceases to make sense. We are not in any particular time and likewise we are not in any particular space; rather than a context of nested physical and social settings, we are in an abstract space. Neither the person nor the place has real coordinates. Normally, each person is located in a number of ways: he or she has distinguishing features as an individual with a character, each has a social role, and communicates with others and the self, in this way bringing together character and role. But in this indiscernible state, the person can merge with others, transform in status and engage in new forms of communication, sharing thoughts and knowledge. In this super-individual state, the predominant emotion can be fear or joy. For these reasons, portrayal of such 'moments' outside time often relate to such conditions as dreams, madness, falling asleep, hypnosis and lucidity (clairvoyance and other powers), and are populated by ghosts and other phantoms such as visitors.

And we are moving in what might be termed a 'primary' space, creating contact with and experiencing what is new and yet, at the same time, eternal because outside the time of sequences. This is contact with the compulsions that organize human life, both an account of the premises of possibility, in terms of quality and power, and experience of the conditions of real change, of the shifting of presuppositions. This is the base matter, constantly changing, of human experience, as it were 'in the raw'. It is, as Deleuze says, a 'state' of expression, not actualization, though it is continually captured and actualized in realistic forms. Virtual forms such as ghosts and their alien confrères link distinct real times and situations through such primary space and time.

It may serve to think of the accounts of visits to craft as taking place in this suspended space and time; the spacecraft have their own non-localized properties, they are nowhere-in-particular. This is true of such visits in abduction narratives, but Adamski's accounts also bear the markings of this state. As Deleuze points out (2001: 100), new forms of transport and new technologies of communication are means of inserting ourselves into time and space, and the improvised details of these visits are largely concerned with creating new forms of distinction, social roles and means of communication to bring back to our temporal lives. We might see these technological devices as switching points, allowing us to transfer out of one social space into a virtual zone, to re-enter normal social life with new properties, transformed. Indeed, new technologies repeatedly summon up ghost-like forms with non-standard properties, modelled for the most part in contemporary versions by substituting wave properties for the physics of solid bodies. But all kinds of communication – writing, recording, radio, radar, television, the Internet – have this property of creating imaginary objects (cf. Peters 1999).

In sum, the expanded interval opens up a virtual space in which feelings – emotions, desires and fears – allow all kinds of new experiences, relationships and other possibilities to emerge. The other way about, this affective delay is the experience of definitional reconfiguration; it is the close-up view on an event in the sense we are using the term. It is analogous to participating in a shift from one state to another – melting, dissolving, boiling, condensing, coagulating – where the part and the whole alter as part of a single process. In such a process, a person involved can run through a series of conditions, can go beyond themselves and join with others, will escape specific time and space coordinates; the process is then separable from any historical sequence. Such a process takes place in a no-man's-land, without geographical markers or reference points. It has qualities – shadows and fears for Barney, light and optimism for Betty – but few details (and those are largely borrowed from clinical medicine). For her, it is possible to make choices in this non-space, so it serves as a place for thought and mental decision. It is possible there to make new connections and create new possibilities (think of all those promised second meetings), but also to make disconnections and separations. This is a space of pure potential, filled with qualities and powers that are quite distinct from any actualization and therefore any time sequence linking past, present and future.

Corresponding external conditions

Events taken as the reconfiguration of relations are marked by anomalies, by parts of the scene that do not fit. A repeated instance is the irregular movement of a light in the sky or a marker on a radar screen which appears to offer evidence of intentional behaviour. There have been many such signs in the materials considered, not only physical, such as lights in the sky, or technical anomalies (the car engine failing, interference in electrical goods such as the radio or television), but also disturbances in formal human relationships at the professional or bureaucratic level, and, less formally, glances or words exchanged between strangers. In each case, we have a sign of mental activity which can either be ignored – attributed to chance in one of many forms – or which provokes the observer to reflection and further enquiry, leading to description and interpretation. As an anomaly, an ordinary object or occurrence can bear both a simple relation, marking a visitor seeking an earthly contact, and an abstract relation, signalling an entire civilization moving into a new phase in its dealings with the earth.

These anomalies at first appear incidental, a disruption in an ongoing story that we understand and, therefore, an episode outside the main action. Yet, they contain the potential to render implausible the overall narrative scheme that underwrites the story of normal life. This is where external factors which might support the disruption of the conventional narrative have their place. Deleuze points out that disconnected, empty spaces of the kind we have been discussing were found in the landscapes of post-War Europe and elsewhere, in the ruins of bomb sites, with entire cities and vast industrial warehouses and docklands laid waste, and that these spaces of nowhere-in-particular were matched by lives that did not make connections, which lacked any secure grounds on which perception could result in confident action, but instead were lived in situations defined by attention paid to sights and sounds, by observation and description. Returning American servicemen had experienced these conditions. Moreover, the American life to which they returned had its comparable factors disrupting any straightforward narrative. These factors appear clearly in pulp stories which describe a range of such features as the mixing of races, reliance on the media for one's opinions, the encompassing power of the built environment and advertising and drugs to shape everyday experience, the hidden nature of authority and power, and the suspicion there was a profound mismatch between appearances and reality, leading to having to distinguish between ambiguous accounts of the work of invisible enemies and the need, precisely, to decipher signs (see Shaver 1945). This condition can be summed up as 'the rise and inflation of images both in the external world and in people's minds' (Deleuze 2001: 206), a condition which had already been described by the techniques of literary modernism in the 1930s, but which became extended to aspects of ordinary post-War life.

This is a transformed world, one which we can no longer believe to be coherent, allowing a defined response to any given situation and capable, too, of being changed by our action; it is therefore one to which the sensory-motor link is no longer the key. Instead, we find a world in which people are only loosely connected, where character and deed often do not match, and where each person gets on with their business. There is no sustained setting to give meaning, such as a unified city or social milieu, nor a given cast of actors; a person may temporarily come to prominence but will then revert to a secondary role or disappear from view. There is no possibility of an agreed common focus or pursuing a project to a conclusion. Indeed, speech and action often no longer connect. Rather, individuals are subject to contingency, making chance encounters, relationships and liaisons, and actions of any kind – 'acts' – may happen almost at random. This is a world made for Existentialism.

In the place of purposeful action, people wander in a space without many markers or reference points. This condition is indeed the starting point for most abduction stories, a car journey of no particular importance in an ill-defined landscape. Among novelists of the period, DeLillo spells out this condition; for example, in *Americana* (DeLillo 1971), a television executive, a dealer in images (and son of an advertising man), sets out on an excursion through deserts and motel rooms to film Indians in Arizona, reflecting a discontinuous world made up entirely of appearances, without sincerity or sustained relations of any kind except commercial interests (cf. Laist 2016).

There are two further features of such a world, following Deleuze, both seeking to create meaning out of such limited order. The first is recourse to cliché. In a dispersive reality without a core, peopled by characters with few connections or features, caught up in events they have neither provoked nor understood, consolidation is provided by 'the current clichés of an epoch or a moment, sound and visual slogans' (Deleuze 2001: 208). The population is fed a mixture of news stories, *faits divers*, advertisements, jingles, songs and images which become mental resources, a part of the interior monologue of each person, 'so that everyone possesses only psychic clichés by which he thinks and feels, [and, indeed,] is thought and received, being himself a cliché among the others in the world which surrounds him' (Deleuze 2001: 208–209). This account contains a good deal of truth about the world of UFOs and exchanges of information about them; there is little that is new or unexpected, no traces of originality.

The second feature is the place of paranoia in organizing and sustaining this internal and external regime of clichés, for it is always possible to suspect there is a powerful organization that produces and circulates the appearances of everyday life and, by doing so, hides itself behind them. Initially, it is thought of as a criminal organization which can only be uncovered piece by piece; this is the work of decipherment. Shaver is typical of the pulp fiction of the period in his belief that the conspiracy can be unmasked and overthrown, that it is possible to get behind appearances, however persuasive and widely shared by modern communications technologies and techniques of advertising, training and pharmaceuticals, and that matters can be righted. Perception and restorative action remain linked. Later versions are more doubtful about this possibility; given the potential of total recording, storage and playback, it is a question whether the invisible marks of editing and falsification can be detected. More, the techniques of mental control go hand in hand with the remodelling of appearances, so that there is potential for intentional manipulation of not only our grasp of present reality but also of our memories and our hopes and desires. No part of the sequence of time is secure. This is the significance of the later appeal to models of psychological warfare and brainwashing, and the struggle between human therapeutic hypnotists and their alien counterparts gives expression to this aspect of the contemporary world condition.

The collapse of modernism

There were considerable differences between the conditions of the Cold War at its height and those of the following two decades; in the 1960s and 1970s the power of the cliché if anything increased, and the focus of paranoid fears moved from primarily external enemies to suspecting deception ever closer to home. Modernist elements became, as it were, increasingly psychologized, moving from being 'out-there' to 'in-here'. It might be possible to relate Keel's waves of sightings to this history, noting what kind of thing was reported at each stage, and linking the appearance of abductions to this transformation. This change in intellectual climate might also appear in the crises that confronted science fiction publishing in the late fifties, including the shift to 'psi' and the disappearance of the pulp market in this period (see Kemp 2011). With regard to our narrow concerns, Shaver described the emerging world with prophetic vigour; Adamski prolonged the realist narrative by focussing on small-scale settings, a characteristic shared by Close Encounters; Keel and Vallee noticed the naivety of this position; and the collapse of the narrative style was completed by the introduction of abductions with their refocussing on the problems of description and memory. This is a move from objects in motion to the mind, a move paralleled in most respects by the project of seeking intelligent contact at distance in SETI, though the move to thought in this instance was wrapped in technical engineering problems.

The world of cliché and paranoia, well described by Dean (1998), Denzler (2001), Lepselter (2016), Pasulka (2019) and others, is not the stopping point, however; the breakdown of the modernist settlement in the 1970s was not an end point but provided the conditions for the emergence of a new position, a different scheme which employs elements from the realist account whilst offering another rationale.[8]

---

8   See Deleuze (2001), chapter 8 for an account of naturalism, chapters 6 and 7 for nowhere-in-particular (not his term), and chapter 12 for the external characteristics corresponding to modernism.

III. Thought rather than action

We now consider signs that lead to thought rather than action. Anomalies both of movement and time become the rule rather than the exception, and the notion of 'lost time' leads us to the use of hypnosis to recover hidden memories and to focus on the detail of work done at the small scale and the circuit or exchange between real and imaginary elements at the heart of the hypnotic session. Again, there are two stages to be considered: the explorations of past time made with the Hills and the innovations introduced by Hopkins.

In the realist account, we find a coherent world made sense of by an integrated protagonist for whom perception is straightforwardly linked to action. In this new world, however, there are no representations that call for immediate response; instead, we look for indications or signs which we have to decipher. More important, these signs when deciphered are not concerned with the real so much as with thought and the mental world; what you see or hear does not lead to action but to reflection, above all, on relations. There may be no reaction possible, simply the realization of a new world condition. In the place of perception and action, we have something like an 'encounter' with its corresponding element being the 'penny dropping': a combination of a new thing and a new mode of registration.

And the protagonist is no longer primarily an actor but a seer, someone who sees, a figure with spirit medium-like properties, responding to an internal vision, recognizing feelings and new relationships – matters of love, recognition, compassion or affliction. We are no longer confronted with an account from the perspective of the individual – 'I see, I decide, I act' – but with a decentred account, where the human character is acted on by the world around and participates in it, lacking the degree of initiative claimed by the first position but, in compensation, with a greater potential for receptivity and sensitivity. The focus has shifted from action to impression, and from an account of moral action based in egoism to one based in compassion (or malice); elsewhere, I have termed this a rhetorical account because of the role it gives persuasion and recognition (Jenkins 2013).

If we consider flying saucer sightings in this perspective, encounter is their central feature: the craft show themselves both to individuals and to groups, at first at a distance, then in ever-closer proximity, with views of machines, glimpses of figures, meetings and, eventually, abductions. In each case, the encounter does not lead to action but to reflection and description; although there are continual attempts to recapture sightings by attributing causes to them in decisive, scientific reports, the crux is in fact the escape from the sensory-motor scheme. In these accounts, the protagonist becomes a spectator, confronted by a vision, recording a sighting without any obvious consequence rather than offering any reaction. And this encounter takes place within the kind of setting we have described, of the trip without purpose within a largely featureless landscape, the multiplication of clichés, the separation of the motivation of events from those to whom they occur.

Two features are associated with this faltering of the action: first, these events happen to marginal people rather than central figures, and second, banality becomes a privileged site for these occurrences, because routines can be readily interrupted. In short, important people and urgent business are rarely interfered with; there is too much invested in the first kind of scheme working for the second kind to emerge.[9]

When observation – seeing, describing – becomes uppermost, objects and settings take on an independent life; we have remarked this.[10] Likewise, we have seen that the business of looking on takes place in a landscape rendered less individual both by banality and a lack of detail, often a desert or a generic countryside. And the characters share with the reader the quality of noticing what goes on; the reader is drawn into the picture and the witness becomes his or her representative because also a spectator. In this regard, the senses are freed up, for we are not trying to get something done – for example, driving from A to B ceases to be a concern – and

9   We might notice that among marginal people in this sense there are few people of colour; although themes of race appear, Barney Hill is an exceptional figure in this regard.
10 This feature may say something about the scope and limits of Object-Oriented Ontology (e.g. Morton 2013).

instead we operate in a dreamlike setting, where environment and action are at best loosely connected.

These dreamlike qualities of passivity, observation and acknowledging can pass over into ordinary life – as, for example, when Adamski's followers spot visitors in hotel lobbies – and the everyday world can in this fashion become a spectacle, but these events then take place in a location which has lost its reference points. These conditions not only resemble dreams but also fantasies and memories from the past.

Under these conditions, we may still be concerned with relations of measurement and distance, seeing the objective relations between figures, for example, or we may be concerned primarily with subjective relations, with feelings (of loyalty and obedience, for instance) and imagination. Yet the strength of the condition derives from the capacity to swap between these poles: real and imaginary, actual and virtual cannot readily be discerned and told apart. Realism can tell you the difference between what is real and what imagined, but under the new conditions, real objects may dissolve or behave outside normal laws, while speech and vision can produce new realities. Mental states create conditions of realization and analysis can alter realities. This is the heart of the matter, from our perspective: not only can Mesmerism, spirits and telepathy offer models for this condition, but so can the life of the modern sciences, with their dialectic of theorized materials and materialized theories. We are dealing with the idea of 'a circuit which exchanges, corrects, selects and sets us off again' (Deleuze 2005: 8), quite distinct from the transmissions of realism from perception to action: we are concerned with signs – of which flying saucers may be an instance – which allow exchanges between the imaginary and the real.

Signs

We can say three things about these signs, or the conditions they share in. They have a focus on everyday life; they allow things, actions, words and so forth to 'speak for themselves'; and they permit their own proper logic – the logic of events – to appear. In this fashion, although they need to be read rather than grasped at first sight, they make time and thought visible. To expand the account a little, the signs allow the grasping of time not as succession but as a simultaneity. What is grasped is excessive, because a quality that cannot be the effect of motor-sensory mechanics, and therefore is unsayable, but it is the emergence into sight of an 'extra dimension', beyond and behind succession. Then, these are signs which demand reading; what is seen has uncanny qualities and breaks down known qualities, and it produces a new kind of character, a visionary (or prophet) who shows rather than tells. We are not dealing in dialogue or explanations or sequences of reasonable actions, but a redeploying of the elements of the real world. We are not separated from the real world but concerned with the emergence of the new in it. We are then, last, concerned in these signs with thought, with the discernment of thought.

These features, Deleuze suggests, give another way of thinking about clichés. We met them as a mechanism for coping with excessive situations, as a means of reducing a reality lacking any clear framework to serve our ends – 'economic interests, ideological beliefs and psychological demands' (Deleuze 2005: 20). But with the incapacity of the sensory-motor scheme, new images (signs) can emerge, beyond metaphor and resemblance, to reveal their necessity and the relations they bear. Clichés can allow sight of the grounds of authority, legitimacy, sovereignty, value and so forth. In short, these signs allow time to be seen, they demand reading, and they discern thought.

This is effectively the agenda set out by Shaver in his pulp stories, who looks at the puzzles of time, of analysis and of discerning patterns of thought. He attempts to decipher what is going on behind appearances, appearances that are made up of actions, clichés, pleasure and consumption. Fed by theosophical sources, he offers several of the tools needed to understand the world as made up of the circulation of the real and the imaginary.

Anomaly becomes the rule

We shift from seeing the world as a theatre for actors and their actions to seeing the world as made up of observers, people to whom things happen and who register change. We may remark in passing the models of language that correlate with these two positions.[11] In the first, language is part of how you cut up the world and reduce the real to something without powers of its own, taking charge and neglecting the role the real plays in differentiating and specifying. In the second, humans use language as they work together on small- or intermediate-scale projects; it is not a straightforward tool used to communicate unambiguous truths. If we take the second condition as more realistic in some regards, we may note that the world never 'gives itself up' to inspection but is always 'being narrated' in one style or another, and that different models of language only operate in the appropriate context.

What are the characteristics of the interval under these new conditions? In the first form, we find time as a succession of moments and, beneath this succession, time as a regular measure (the interval) and as the totality of intervals. In this first regime, novelty emerges as an anomaly, when the measure ceases to serve and the notion of a secure point of observation – making sense of each moment, playing the conscious part with respect to the whole – becomes confused. The second kind of regime may be seen in the perspective of the anomalous becoming the rule, the disappearance both of the measure and of the background against which we use it to make sense. It is worth recalling that flying saucers appeared initially as aberrant movement, with their ability to accelerate and to stop dead, to reverse direction, to disappear and reappear, to move to another site and then return; they make us doubt the laws of physics.

Once the anomaly comes to prominence, the present moment ceases to be self-evident and to serve as the pivot through which time passes. We are pushed instead to a set of concerns about time, some of them quite commonplace, others less so. When confronted with a person such as Adamski, we need to learn who he was and to place him; we follow his development, chart the results of his choices and discern aspects of his character. In this regard, the story he tells disappears into a series of temporal frames: a system of teaching and its transmission, semi-formal institutions and their histories, networks of people, meetings and situations, not to mention redactions and dissemination and so forth, together with the unfolding

---

11 These models are discussed in the fourth essay, *UFO Reports*.

of relations between these elements. Time in a certain sense – not in the sense of succession – becomes primary, the medium within which lives are lived and which can appear for itself, as the condition to which memory can allow access. We are dealing in a 'dimension where people and things occupy a place in time which is incommensurate with the one they have in space' (Deleuze 2005: 38).

If aberrant movement then is a sign of the shift in scheme with which we are concerned, it likewise marks the appearance of a discontinuity in time, a break, presenting the emergence of the new as such, caught in its pristine condition, without cover or alibi. In abductions, this discontinuity is marked by the phrase 'lost time', denoting a cut in the succession of episodes of ordinary life.

Lost time (1) the Hills

The mode of observation and description therefore implies a different account of time and memory. Because the anomalous object under consideration demands thought rather than allowing the kind of ready recognition that results in response in the realist scheme, the observer has to return to the object repeatedly, seeking each time to identify different features and so working through a series of recognitions as he or she grasps different aspects. In each case, recognition implies recollection, but in the first case, memory is a replication of the real, while in the second, it explores different depths of the past and connections. The one is a utilitarian, abstract act of classification – 'this is an instance of x' (and good for the following purpose) – while the other is personal and an exploration of the singularity of the thing in question and its placing with respect to other things.

Just as the pragmatic needs of the realist scheme continually cover over anomalies and inconsistencies for practical ends, so too there are ways in which the sequential memories employed by realism both break down and are recuperated. We can see the interactions between the psychiatrist Simon and the Hills in the light of these processes (see Fuller 1966b). Memories reach into the past and are, by this characteristic, virtual rather than actual, imaginary rather than real. Yet, by their therapeutic recovery, they may return to serve present purposes. Fuller believed that, in recollection, the past can be re-run like a film, re-wound and re-shown, and so returned to consciousness. This may be compared with Simon's more sophisticated account that memories – and he does not discriminate between true and false memories – are employed in the present to do work, and that they effect change for good or ill. It is then the therapist's task to help the patient use virtual memories to serve actual ends, to relieve anxiety and to return to normal functioning.

Both attitudes recuperate the past to present ends, one assuming a literal past that once was present, the other undecided about the status of the recovered past but still relating it to past real events as their projection and transformation. Such recuperation of memories can involve direct recollection, and reliving episodes (flashbacks, recovered under hypnosis), and dreams. All three were employed in Betty Hill's treatment. But at the same time, a new subjectivity emerged through these sessions, not leading to the recovery of the practical person who existed prior to the encounter so much as marking the appearance of a new, reflective personality whose horizons had altered and who rejected the doctor's proffered explanation – that Betty had passed her dreams by suggestion to Barney. In this second perspective, each recovered memory represents a choice, a junction in the path with one outcome discarded and the other track taken. This is not a linear narrative, a sequence of options, but demands that the nested, discontinuous decisions be thought of as simultaneous, for each choice implicates all the others; we are mapping a single process of becoming something new, the emergence of the Betty Hill known to ufologists. The task of recovered memory is to ask, what happened? And how did we get to this point? The therapeutic process is the constitution of a new subject and a new voice (cf. Bender 2010 on the creation of New Age subjectivity).

We can take this analysis further when considering the work of Hopkins (1981, 1987) and Strieber (1987) on recovered memory. For the moment, let us notice that, by presenting us with Simon's recordings, Fuller gives a clue as to the mechanism of production of the new subject and voice. As readers, we watch the constitution of the new person: we see the gap between what was seen and what was reported and the contradictions between the two, and the process of construction of a new experience between them. We see Simon's role in constituting the framework which allows Betty as medium to produce her voice and articulate the invisible world that she can see, and we share Fuller's part in the work as audience. It is this threefold relation of medium, producer and audience (Betty Hill, Simon and Fuller/the reader) which allows this circulation between experience and re-writing the rules to occur, without leading to action, and the relation takes place in the suspended delay created by the interaction of sighting and report.

Rather than dealing in the recovery of conscious memory that has become obscured, as Fuller believed, we are concerned with failure of memory and with its disturbances; we are concerned with such mental phenomena as 'amnesia, hypnosis, hallucination, madness ... and especially nightmares and dreams' (Deleuze 2005: 53). In these psychic states, the protagonist is subject to contradictory sensations – sights and sounds – that do not lead to recognition and ready action. Barney was simultaneously fascinated and frightened, he felt both threat and reassurance, he fled by an act of will but was overcome and mastered in a moment subsequently. And in this condition, although he mobilized the occasional memory – recalling seeing a hunted animal, perhaps recollecting a recent television series – by and large, his mental state was detached from specific recollections and the potential for reaction. Once abducted, his mental condition became that of relaxation, detachment and an impression of floating. This state matches that in which memory is 'recovered': hypnosis detaches the patient from their sensory-motor condition and repeats the abduction situation. Rather than replaying a recording and recovering exact memories of the past, it allows floating memories of earlier episodes to come into view in a fragmentary fashion, a chain of repetitions organized around the recovery of time, without implications for action and allowing new insights and descriptions.

The Hills were poised on a boundary between the two schemes. Recollections, a dream-like world, the sense of a generalized past, dream images, fantasies, promptings of various kinds, all relate to a new subjectivity and the failure of the action scheme. But in all the analyses, both Simon's and Fuller's, the premise is that we return to the real, via a circuit involving dreams, recovered memories and conscious recollection. The signs, including lost time, are taken to point to a lost reality. In this recovered world the visitors become natural forces supplementing and restoring the faltering character of the abductee, who needs to make decisions only when confronted with the re-telling. The world then loses any dreamlike properties it might have had; having taken front place, the virtual dimension retreats into the background and becomes subordinate to actuality.

Lost time (2) Hopkins

The parallels with the séance become pronounced in Hopkins' development of the abduction scenario. In it, the therapeutic session re-enacts in miniature the history of the abduction. And the dislocation between the actual performance of the various actors and what is said becomes extreme.

We have seen in the Simon-Hills sessions how the therapist searched through the recollections, recovered memories and, eventually, the dreams of the Hills, going ever further afield, searching levels of the past in order to bring these elements into contact with the present of the session and the ordinary lives of the patients. The audience, other than the therapist, was not present except in the recordings made, listened to subsequently by Simon, then played to the Hills and, eventually to Fuller and passed on to us, the readers. When we turn to the sessions organized by Hopkins, we find a more developed scenario much akin to a spiritualist séance, with not only a medium – the abductee – and an operator – the therapist/hypnotist – but also an audience – Hopkins and his colleague – able actively to participate. These three parties together enable the abductee to reproduce a virtual world with its own cast of actors. The key relation at the heart of the session is the re-enactment of the abduction, as it were for its own sake. We have a duplication: the actual relations of the session and the virtual relations of the encounter are brought into the same space, a minimal unit, where the reflection cannot be told apart from the original. We swap from one to the other. Rather than searching through dreams, recovered memories and recollections to reattach them to the present – the past in the present – we can observe the mechanism, the minimal unit, by which the past and the present are produced together, a direct sight of time as change, rather than an indirect seizing of time as a sequence of past moments leading to the present.

In these sessions the abduction becomes real and then goes virtual again, just as flying saucers are sighted and vanish. 'It is as if an image in a mirror ... came to life, assumed independence and passed into the actual, even if this meant that the actual image returned into the mirror and resumed its place ... following a double movement of liberation and capture' (Deleuze 2005: 67). This is the scale at which the sign produces its effects, as it allows the real and the imaginary, the physical and the mental, to follow one another and to exchange qualities. Each remains distinct but, in the event, indiscernible, 'each side taking the other's role in a relation which we must describe as reciprocal presupposition, or reversibility' (Deleuze 2005: 68). This is not an effect produced in the mind and attributable to confusion or psychology; it is an objective characteristic of the second kind of scheme, effective under defined circumstances.

In this type of exchange, without confusion of kinds, each party gains new properties because of the relationship, though properties which are neither latent nor imitated.[12] In the process of exchange, the real actors become virtual players during the session, the 'real' self being simply one option in a series of virtual possibilities; as they exchange qualities, the imagined actors gain solidity and clarity while their real counterparts become opaque and shadowy, and there are reversals between the authority, roles and spiritual powers of the various participants (Strieber portrays this feature particularly). These kinds of exchanges are close to those effected between the living and the dead in spiritualist séances. We might say the dead can only find expression through the living, but the living also gain new qualities and powers through the encounter; it is no different with the encounter with visitors.

Re-enactment in this sense, the replication of the encounter in its essentials without any additional features, is then the means of producing the abduction; it is an act of miniaturization, a play within the play.

---

12   This type of exchange was outlined in the last chapter of the fourth essay, *UFO Reports*.

Time in a different perspective

Can we be more precise in how this act of miniaturization, this doubling up, works? The therapeutic session in which memory is recovered allows the past to coexist with the present; the business of recollection is contemporary with the present perception. This, in Bergson's term, is 'pure recollection', existing outside the time of consciousness; it is 'the past as it is in itself' (Deleuze 2005: 78), before it becomes actualized as specific memories, located in a sequence and so marked as 'past'. The session is the means of producing this minimal unit, a present and its own past, where actual and virtual cannot be told apart. The realist scheme is the means by which life introduces indeterminacy (in the form of the actor's decisions) into the transmissions of physical cause and effect, while the second scheme realizes that real and imaginary cannot be discerned apart when focussing on the nature of time. Indeterminacy in the first as compared with indiscernibility in the second.

If, in the realist scheme, the interval is the minimum delay between reception and response, in the second scheme the interval has become this operation which splits 'the present into two heterogeneous directions, one of which is launched towards the future while the other falls into the past' (Deleuze 2005: 78–79). In this scheme, as time unrolls it is divided into one stream which makes the present pass on and another which preserves the past. What we find in the session, as the smaller unit replicating the larger process, is 'the perpetual foundation of time, non-chronological time' (Deleuze 2005: 79).

In the first scheme, time as sequence is underwritten by time as two kinds of limit: the smallest interval and the greatest sum, the present moment and the cosmos. In the second scheme, we find simultaneous time as the virtual point of production of present and past and as the whole, the past in general. Time in this regard is not over in a moment but 'the virtual image of the past which is preserved' (Deleuze 2005: 79). What are we to make of this account of time as not only the simultaneous production of past and present, but also the non-real preservation of the past, the virtual presence of the past which can, on occasion, be reached or made accessible?

In Deleuze's view, this is time conceived as the movement of images that composes the world. We might describe it as time 'before' it becomes time as sequence; time as event or judgement, as Kairos not Chronos. And the subject who recovers memories, the medium or seer, is what elsewhere we have termed a 'prophet' (Jenkins 2013), one who 'sees' the event for what it is, the emergence of a new order of thought in the happenings of the present: both novelty and registration in a new mode. In this visionary perspective, the prophet inhabits non-chronological time. Time is not interior subjectivity, our internal life, but the milieu in which we live and move and have our being. This condition is only occasionally glimpsed, for normally we subject it to various reductions for pragmatic ends. But the therapeutic session does the work that occurs elsewhere with the collapse of second order categories: time appears clearly for itself, giving access to the mind-like movements of the totality and to the fulness of the restored past.[13]

To what extent does this re-enactment give access to the restored past? By and large, incompletely, and the story rarely ends well. In the examples we have of prophecy, the exchanges of distinct images, real and imaginary, leads fast or slow to crisis and collapse. We might say three things about such accounts in general. First, that because of the presence of hidden figures, ambiguous messages and so forth, life becomes considered as a performance; the gap between the real story and appearances becomes exaggerated. And second, the performance is largely made up of repetitions; we go to and fro between the present and the past, without resolution. Those two features are marks of abduction stories and explain why they make such uncomfortable reading, for there appears to be no way out. Yet, on occasion, some opportunity arises that allows the participant to escape from these repetitions. This escape may be by violence, which is a present possibility throughout; a breakdown of order, sometimes through the discovery of dark forces within the family, often through outside intervention, orchestrated

---

13   This Bergsonian account bears many parallels with Durkheim's exploration in *The Elementary Forms* of the generation of collective representations through collective effervescence, producing representations with the power to effect comparison and abstraction. This is a description of the production of Mind through the experience of plenitude and excess beyond the individual.

by press interest. Sometimes, however, positive opportunities are created by improvisation, trying out new roles and opening back into ordinary life. The survivors' groups can play a role of this kind. Many abductees after a while refuse the repetitions of the sessions and simply escape back into a previous way of life, while others, such as Betty Hill, construct a new life out of the experience. She might be said to have taken the future path rather than the past; such choices have political dimensions, as Lepselter's accounts indicate (Lepselter 2016). In short, touching the past, the recovery of original time, can be seen as a resource for either progress or decline. The third characteristic is the sense that something – be it a realization or resolution, such as a sense of interconnection between the elements – always arrives too late: understanding is retrospective, and that while it may be reparative, it cannot undo what is done.

IV. Recovered memories

In this penultimate section, we develop the account of pure recollection that emerged in considering the hypnotic session, understood as a mechanism creating a circuit between the real and the imaginary. The new person created in the session – the abductee's remembering self – returns to different layers of the past, providing materials for those sharing the investigation to discern an event, significant change active in the present. We consider in turn the role played by that new person, parallels between their work of making sense and wider situations, and the place of the relation between sightings and reports in these productions.

Two aspects of non-chronological time

Hopkins' investigation of recovered memories has three innovations. First, the discovery that one needs no special event, no remembered encounter, to prompt investigation, but only the location by a second party, the investigator, of a period of missing time in the life of the subject, to justify seeking to get behind the obstacle of amnesia and recover the hidden memories. Second, the discovery not of a single lost event but of a series of such events at different points in the past, each caught up in the earlier and later disclosures, so that we find a series of interlocking events or switches in the direction of the subject's life. And third, the discovery that these histories involve more than a single person's life; that whole families and separate generations are part of the same story.[14] In Hopkins' investigations we find revision and recapturing hither-to forgotten moments, a steady extension of the process ever-further into the past, recalling other incidents of lost time, and extension too into the lives of others.

What are the implications of these innovations for the understanding of time which has emerged? The structure of the therapeutic session makes clear the hidden ground of time with its two simultaneous productions of presents which pass and of pasts which are preserved. Memory, rather than being something personal within us, is the medium in which we move and seek the 'seeds' of the past which allow recollection. Once a period of lost time is located, a sign which demands repeated reflection, the abductee – with assistance – returns to different circles or depths of the past, each level with its own characteristics, aspects, singular points and dominant themes. In this perspective, the present is simply the most concentrated form in which we encounter this wider form of time as a series of depths, just as the individual is the point of transfer between social fields and collective representations. The present of the session is this limit point, 'the smallest circuit that contains all the past' (Deleuze 2005: 96). And in this present, all the circles of the past are contained simultaneously. Hence

---

14   We should note that all these features appear in spiritualist histories, for example, Theobald (1884). We find retrospective insight into earlier spirit guidance, the significance of which may, indeed, only appear in the afterlife; a sequence of such promptings in the life of an enquirer, which form their education, including the gradual revelation of the second world parallel to this one, a process which can only be seen for what it is after the subject's 'conversion'; and the engagement of the extended family group, both living and dead, in these intermittent narratives.

the ability of the abductee to pass from recent incidents to more distant ones, to recover memories from childhood and even, on occasion, memories from before birth. These, in Deleuze's summary, 'are the paradoxical characteristics of a non-chronological time: the pre-existence of a past in general; the coexistence of all the sheets of the past; and the existence of a most contracted degree' (Deleuze 2005: 96). It is the virtual medium, the form of pre-existence, in which we place ourselves in order to make sense, to recover time, to read signs and to find intelligence (or thought) at work.

Recovered memories are then actualized out of this milieu in recollections of specific places and times. In this perspective, rather than a series of layers of time, pure recollection takes the form of a series of interconnected events, a set of significant moments which gives birth to a second person within the first, a person whose memories, understanding and desires have been altered because of the connections formed, and who therefore lacks clear identity or boundaries, who cannot be assimilated to the first but who is defined by the process at work.[15] We might note that, while narration of this process is possible, it does not relate to successive actions but to a simultaneous set of possibilities or potentials: the distribution of implicated presents, their revision, contradiction, obliteration, substitution and re-creation. And the 'character' involved – the second person – not only makes choices, taking one fork in the path rather than another (cf. Deleuze 2005: 98), but can also return and make another choice, inconsistent with the first. We have a series of presents each of which is possible but are not all compatible. One can imagine the same recovered instance can play out differently in repetitions, as one returns reiteratively to the layers of the past, being realized in incompatible versions, and there is no way of resolving which version is 'true'.

There are then two faces to time in this second scheme dealing in non-chronological time: time as layers of the past and time as 'event', as these pathways in which every part relies on all the others. This is a different idea to time conceived as succession in the first scheme, with its underlying concepts of time as measure and time as the totality of intervals. This

---

15 This account has parallels with accounts of the work of prayer in the Christian tradition (see Cugno 1982).

second pair is set free by the repetitions and variations of the therapeutic session, which allows the subject to break with time's subordination to movement and sequence. In this new account, we find either 'a plurality of simultaneous worlds [our layers] … [or] a simultaneity of presents in different worlds' (Deleuze 2005: 100). The session allows a different construction of time, of remembering and of forgetting.

Work done within the session

In the session of regression under hypnosis, recovered memories then point to different presuppositions to those undergirding ordinary life, a different kind of existence. The business of recollection gives clues to the conditions that make it possible. The time of abductions is unremarkable, banal and even idle, filled with habitual activities and marked by lack of purpose; the Hills' holiday journey is typical in this regard. The things that happen begin out of sight and are first seen only out of the corner of the eye, coming into prominence out of the background as an anomalous light or sudden sound. In this fashion, ordinary space and time become transformed, penetrated by this freed time which is signalled by something seen or heard, to which there is no reaction possible other than paying attention; the conditions both of the outside world and inside the mind – registration of the environment – have altered in no time at all.

Although they are often presented as recalling something that happened and has been forgotten, recovered memories in fact contain a more complex process of interpretation. Each search moves between the variations of the pure past, going back to different layers and forth to the contractions of the present, the revelation of significance. And the development of the latter, exploring the nature and implications of the event, then allows the search to be renewed, returning to another level of the past. In each repetition, we get not only developments and new perspectives, but different versions, in which first perceptions are revised or even contradicted and replaced.

We might notice that there is never a final, agreed account of an abduction, let alone of one of the complex histories of multiple persons, for each recurrence tells of its concerns from a different angle, arguing from a different depth of time. And this condition bears an analogy with flying saucer sightings, from which no consistent system of classification emerges. Unlike manmade rockets and aeroplanes, we cannot class sightings by appearances; there are no 'makes' of flying saucer, despite efforts to define some in the early days. This failure to classify types of unidentified craft corresponds in this regard to the condition of recovered memories.

Because of these ambiguous conditions, there are many things that can go wrong in these efforts of remembering. The recovered pasts may make no contribution to the present, either because they were sterile moments or because the present has become so different as to render their contribution useless; it may be too late. Or, the past may not be recoverable, and recollection proves impossible. Or, again, it may be that the amnesia cannot be overcome and all we produce are fictions. Despite the hope recovered memory holds out of gaining access to suppressed truthful recollection, its practices suggest more there is only a pre-existing chaos without strong causal links, and that the best we can achieve are short chains of sense-making.

We might suggest, put crudely, that, corresponding to the residual optimism of the ufologist and the positivist mindset that we shall make sense of reality (the man of truth), there is an equivalent pessimism of the one who sees the mysteries of time with a clearer eye (the seer or medium, who deals in things that are hidden). It is possible to live well in such a second world, but only at the price of a certain gnosticism – a dualism of mind and body – and mysticism – a commitment to there being an overall order, which we wait upon to show itself. It is a question, to which we will return, as to whether there is an alternative to both positions; whether, instead of seeking a definite truth that is always either delayed (optimists) or obscured (pessimists) – a search which tends to end in death in one form or another – we can live in the meantime with a world made up of the interfaces between different holders of memory, constructed through the undecidable alternatives between layers of the past and expression in events.

Hopkins is more interested in the discontinuities of the event and the hidden links it creates which allow a new life to hatch under the old than he is in the constantly devised interplay of layers, going back repeatedly into the past to find new resources in the others with whom one interacts. The task of hypnosis, in this perspective, is to return the client/abductee to different time levels, while Hopkins' job is to reconstruct the overall event. The anthropological task might be seen as balancing the two aspects of pure time, exploring biographies, itineraries, spaces and places in order to mark the moments when the penny drops, when we can be connected to the fulness of the past that normally escapes us and placed back in that particular past. Through mapping and the reconstruction of relationships we approach the mental functions and levels of thought that constitute the subject matter of anthropology, the transformations of totalities at different scales and interaction of initially distinct zones and times. The task is, then, more making an inventory of multiple mappings of the world than privileging any one account or way through, and, on that basis, to tell the story of how these different accounts arose and interact, as the recovered moments of full description communicate one with another. The last task of the anthropologist is to construe the logic of the events described – that is the task both of this series as a whole and of this essay – and so in a sense to recover lost time. In short, make an inventory, tell the story, describe the logic.

What is the true subject matter of this process of description? We might say feelings, in the sense of recollections at work in the past, not the psychology of the actors involved but the circulation of feelings between levels of the past, according to each transformation. These feelings, Deleuze says, appear in each character, but can only be revealed by hypnosis: 'it is hypnosis which reveals thought to itself' (Deleuze 2005: 120).

The differences between regimes

Deleuze offers a summary of the differences between the two regimes, concerning their distinct notions of description, of the relation between the real and the imaginary, and of narration. This summary leads to a discussion of the kind of character who emerges in accounts of synchronous time, the second person who emerges within the first and who allows transfers of properties between the visitors and the human seeker. We turn first to the principal features of the summary.

In the first place, the two schemes mean something different by description. In the realist account, we assume a pre-existing, independent object, while, in the other, description 'stands for its object, replaces it, both creates and erases it ... and constantly gives way to other descriptions which contradict, displace, or modify the preceding ones' (Deleuze 2005: 122). We no longer imagine a record of stimulus and response, as Fuller does, but see the task in terms of conveying the significance of observing and seeing, of grasping the import of a moment, an event, a shift in the ordering of perception. We have moved from a concern with the priority of bodies and their actions to the priority of mind and time.

Then, each contains a different account of the relationship between the real and the imaginary. In the first regime, reality is continuous and consistent, following laws and regular successions; you can locate relations, make links and deduce logical connections. In this regime, the imaginary – recollection, dream, imagination – appears in contrast to the real; it is marked by discontinuity with the real, and does not have to be consistent, law bound and made up of logical sequences. These capricious imaginary forms appear in the conscious mind and, in practice, do so 'in accordance with the needs of the present actual or the crises of the real' (Deleuze 2005: 123). These are 'non-existent objects' (Crane 2013). In the second regime, their relation is quite different, for the real no longer operates as securely and independently as it did, and the imaginary gains autonomy. The two modes instead combine in a circuit (as we saw in the session), where they 'chase after each other, exchange their role and become indiscernible' (Deleuze 2005: 123).

Third, the two regimes offer different kinds of narrative. The first claims to be true and to take place in a measurable space, a place where 'characters react to situations or act in such a way to disclose the situation' (Deleuze 2005: 124). In such a space, predictions are possible (cf. Jenkins 2013): one can predict the outcome of a given situation because certain rules hold, the laws of efficient action, for example, so that one can anticipate an opponent will deploy the minimum effort required to achieve her desired end, and so can thwart her or, retrospectively, detect and reconstruct her crime. Movements and actions are distributed in space by known and localized actors and ordered by a simple succession. Under these conditions, various forms of disorder – interruptions, recollections, dreams or acts of imagination – are simply surface disturbances; they do no more than camouflage the underlying order, and an experienced person can see past them.

A different kind of narrative arises in the second regime. Signs are given, in the form of sightings or messages, to which the recipients can offer no direct response; instead, they need to understand the problem, to see its terms and to reconfigure their picture of the world. In place of regular movement, attention is focussed on anomalies, for anomalies point to the failure of a homogeneous space of distributed and attributed actions and so to the shaking of the entire system of classification. Physical anomalies point to a shift in the terms of a problem, to an event in the strong sense, an altered optic of registration. Under these conditions, we find overlapping perspectives which are incompatible but without priority, a state as it were 'before' any consistent space: the conditions call attention to the presuppositions needed for ordinary space to operate. And the mind hesitates between perspectives rather than making any kind of straightforward choice between simple objects or directions.

This is a (non-) narrative of simultaneous time when, as we have seen, one moves between interconnected moments of decision (a singularity, an event) and ever-deeper layers of the past. Because she is selecting between incompatible versions where one perspective can stand in for another, with different outcomes, the 'actor' is necessarily dealing in multiple possibilities, where one position effectively denies another. She is faced with different paths, where each choice renders a different past likely and gives a different account of the present. In these circumstances, narration becomes 'fundamentally falsifying' (Deleuze 2005: 127); it is concerned with striking out previously granted suppositions (cf. Bachelard's account of a 'philosophy of no' – Bachelard 1940).

In this account, the session gives rise to descriptions and to nothing else; 'description becomes its own object' (Deleuze 2005: 128), and each narration lays out a story of succession through time and simultaneously denies the truth claims of that chosen path. This second style of story will equally have its 'ready-made formulas, its set procedures, its laboured and empty applications, its failures, its conventional and "second-hand" examples' (Deleuze 2005: 128) to distract us, but its dominant motifs are 'events' (in the strong sense), multiple life forms rather than individuals, and the work of the imagination, or the virtual condition.

The role of the medium

In this second kind of account, the abductee as seer or medium has come to prominence; this is the person whom the hypnotic session allows to work as a maker of pure descriptions, making visible synchronous time. In realistic descriptions, the medium may be present but always as a minor figure, and it is worth remarking the unacceptable nature of such a person in the first regime: it is because 'he provokes undecidable alternatives and inexplicable differences between the true and the false, and thereby imposes a power of the false as adequate to time, in contrast to any form of the true which would control time' (Deleuze 2005: 128). Put into English, in the hypnotic session the abductee takes on the role of presenting a variety of recovered accounts; he or she falsifies one version after another, leaving us unclear as what to believe. Because of the unreliability of the second personality, this character may be seen in the perspective of the first regime as a counterfeiter, an imposter, a charlatan or a confidence trickster.

We observe a series of substitutions. In the session, the abductee gains a second, remembering personality, and this personality enters into relationships with the equivalent of a spirit control, the alien who has become individuated, and we learn the possibility of seeing from its point of view, its seeking after 'communion'. Strieber's account brings out these substitutions with great clarity. Through this chain of 'abductee – second personality – alien', there is communication of properties from the alien, as representative of its community, to the abductee, as representative of theirs, and, presumably, reciprocal exchange. It is this combined figure, the second personality with relations in both directions, who brings together real and imaginary (actual and virtual) and who offers alternative readings. It is this relationship with the alien that allows healing and the redressing of some wrongs as well as the perpetration and prolonging of others, and which marks the shift from action to observation on the part of the encountering party.

This chain of metamorphoses of characters brings certain consequences with which we are familiar. The rules of truthful narration, of testimony and some sort of juridical tribunal or testing, do not apply. And the investigator, the hypnotist and other secondary witnesses are implicated just as much as the person testifying to their abduction in the narrative of disconnected places and moments abstracted from linear time. More, nobody involved has a simple, well-bounded identity, instead becoming one of a chain of personalities which overlap and merge. We are dealing in multiples rather than individuals. This is exemplified by the hive mind of the insect-like aliens (see Strieber 1987), but it also reflects the representative nature of the abductee; each is simply a contact point between multiplicities for the purposes of interaction, making new qualities emerge in each population. And, because of the power of revision, the chains of metamorphoses are not single but multiple; different relations and different interactions may emerge in different alternative histories.

What are the consequences of such a regime? What kind of world do we find, populated by these figures without any core, what kinds of character emerge, and what possibility is there of their coming to some sort of good? We have seen that judgement becomes impossible and that we can no longer have a concept of a truthful person nor a truthful world. Hypnosis of course was meant to be a way of finding the truth and allowing judgements to be made, but it does not succeed in escaping the labyrinth of its own making. And when the real world goes down, we lose with it any possible account of a world of appearances.

What we are left with are bodies, abducted, experimented on, manipulated, investigated, even copulated with on occasion. Here we meet with the naturalism Keel recognized (Keel 2013): the expression of instincts and, in particular, the need to dominate on the part of the aliens and the need to be recognized on the part of their human victims. These are two figures of the will to power, engaged in a morbid competition leading to death. This is one aspect that makes the abduction narratives so disturbing.

Strieber however signals the possibility of another mode of being within this scheme, one that transcends this competition for limited resources and opens on to the creation of new values, when he invokes Gurdjieff and Ouspensky with the talk of symbols and triads and the mutual liberation of alien- and humankind. Unsurprisingly, we have little detail on how these concerns might return to the sphere of ordinary life, returning to the real with different resources, living without centres, without laws, without any confining accounts of truth. It might be possible to construe Lepselter's ethnography in this light, as people who escape both the traps of known truths and the eventual fate of those engaged on the pathways of metamorphosis (Lepselter 2016). Yet theirs is a life balanced on a knife edge, between the traps posed by 'truthful men' – scientists or ufologists – and the 'confidence tricksters' with their stories of abduction: both seek to turn the experience of simultaneous time, the emergence of the new, into copies and models, into forms that can be controlled and manipulated.

The medium's work in a wider context

The hypnotic session offers three striking features in comparison with the first scheme. We begin with a discontinuity in time, a break which destroys any possible unity and coherence of man and the world. With the obliteration of the whole and its causal links, all we have for making sense is the dislocation between images and the possibility of drawing together 'a sequence of mental states' (Deleuze 2005: 168). And, likewise, we lose any possibility of an internal monologue, a narrative told herself by the protagonist (which we might overhear). Instead, the protagonist takes on the role of medium, finding herself a third party caught in relationships she did not choose and initiatives she has no control over, speaking words and behaving as if she were another person, participating in processes which are dominated by clichés and of which she is able only to recall fragments.

As Strieber in particular suggests, it is still possible to operate within such a world, to work with what is seen and heard, to propose theories as to what is happening and to attempt to meet the problems the events raise. But the main ethical question for the abductee is the larger one of whether to act as a believer in this situation or, on the contrary, to reject the whole premise: whether to accept there is another world beyond and within this one or to fight to restore the former order. There is a possible range, too, among those who respond positively; perhaps the most restrictive option is only to choose once and to be caught by a single decision, while the most liberating is to make repeated choices and revisions, to be flexible enough to avoid the various traps that await. There are parallels with the uses of automatism – trance and automatic writing – in Spiritualism and in early Surrealism.

The anthropological task

A good part of this model of creativity mimics that of the novelist, the writer of fiction. The generative force in the hypnotic sessions is not the force of the whole, as it is in the first, realist scheme, where coherence and connections between parts does the work, but differences between images and the production of new elements which in turn serve to produce further differences. This is the process of repeated correction and replacement found in the searching through layers of memory, in the most general formulation, the generative differences between sightings (or encounters) and reports. The world impinges on thought in these accounts as unthought, as irrational, but not, for that, negligible or not existing.

The anthropological task is not altogether different to the novelist's. It seeks to put together the nature of change and the resources mobilized in a specific instance by giving the story of those involved, telling the before and the after, so as to focus on the interval, the generative force at work in the moment under consideration. As we have seen, there are a number of ways of doing this. In the first scheme, we start off with a witness and what he sees and try, after investigation and reading reports, to recover what happened and reconstruct the subject's reasons; in this perspective, scenario and experience should match up. Yet in practice, investigation shows that different witnesses produce irreconcilable reports and that the presence of investigators multiplies the possibilities. And when we turn to accounts of abductions, repeated sessions of hypnosis produce the same effect within a single witness, who has herself doubled up, producing a host of incompatible perspectives. In this process, we move from the idea of a single truthful account to a set of perspectives and, finally, to stories for which the question of truthfulness is not their primary interest. And the character of the witness changes from truthful to fabulous, or rather, to be more precise, in the latter cases the two figures form a circuit and exchange roles back and forth: we can never be sure who is speaking.

This process of exchange is the mechanism which allows the interpenetration of real and imaginary, which is the conundrum at the heart of the problem of flying saucers. The hypnotic session represents an accessible instance of a mechanism that is far more widespread and is at work in the various phenomena of things sighted, with their powers of communicating at a distance, acting as relay between times and places, their ability to connect and separate persons, to disturb social forms and produce both short-lived and lasting effects of an unpredictable kind. Indeed, many writers have discussed these phenomena in a far wider range of settings, describing how interactions between images give rise to new forms and information.[16]

In all these accounts, we find the same concerns as have emerged in our investigation. Truth claims cease to hold first place in making a description, and making reports has the power to affect real conditions. The characters of the various participants are altered through the processes being investigated; they have a 'before' and an 'after'. And this effect extends to others taking part; the investigator and, by implication, the person recording the history (and therefore possibly even the reader) are changed by the encounter.[17] These features together point to a social process of production, the production of new effects through works of the mind and their metamorphoses which break their bounds and affect wider populations.

---

16 In addition to Deleuze and Bachelard, one could mention Stengers and Prigogine (1997), Simondon's concept of 'transduction' (1989) and Méheust's notion of 'description-production' (1999 I: 82–106). Méheust is particularly valuable because he focusses on debates between hypnotists and mesmerists concerning 'lucid' powers – action at a distance, foresight, travelling, healing and so forth.

17 Lest one think these considerations do not apply to scientific topics, we only have to recall that every significant advance bears the name of its discoverer or is strongly associated with that name.

The witnesses and their interlocutors cease to be either right or engaged in fictions; rather, they become all the more real as they invent themselves and overcome limits.

We have an account of how, under certain conditions, the mind is capable of making new connections and new mappings of the real. The categories of truth are, to this extent, historical, and this gives a handle to the most surprising feature of mental phenomena, that they appear in some respects to be called up by the theories which claim to describe them. In this fashion, phenomena of the kind we are pursuing renew the principal problem to their being grasped in a clear fashion and retain their capacity to surprise the theorist.

Under these conditions, what might be construed as negative features – the disappearance of unity both at the personal and the cosmic levels, the evaporation of finding forms of harmony, figures and metaphor, and the prominence of banality and cliché – give way because they can provide the material for active speech, when speech can describe real conditions and all concerned may share in certain common problems, not working at a large scale of mastering, deciding and solving, but at a smaller scale participating in difficulties and passions. We are not masters of the universe, but we are confronted with woes and joys against a human horizon.

Fiction is then, in Deleuze's words, 'a power not a model' (Deleuze 2005: 147) and can be understood as a mode of practical action undertaken in the milieu of non-chronological time. The characters continually pass between the real and fiction, and the anthropologist tracks their transformations through their repeated actions and the associated work done with the wider groups who are implicated. It is here that one can situate the political themes identified both by Dean (1998) and Lepselter (2016), though I shall not pursue that direction. In this perspective, I suggest, rather, that the anthropologist fulfils the novelist's function, acting as 'a writer without a "message", either philosophical, religious or political … content to examine without comment, and to illustrate through character in action, the changes in human nature brought about by the changing face of the social order in which we live' (Maclaren-Ross 2005: 325).

Sighting and report

A final note on the role of language in the separation we find between report and sighting, given the independence that has arisen between what is said and what is seen and their potential for cooperation or conflict.

On the most straightforward model, language describes what is there; it gives information, saying what has been seen. While what is seen is singular and natural, or real, language allows us to make sense of it by mapping what is seen in terms of generalities, even universals, in this fashion invoking culture and the law, in terms of what can be said and what cannot. But, as we have seen, in practice reports open up differences and mark conflicts in interpretation.

So, even on this most straightforward model, we find a dislocation between sight and speech. And this is more generally the case; in any social encounter, the actors say little of what they observe or what they think and, indeed, conversation normally communicates banalities or even attempts to misdirect attention, to conceal the objectives and desires of the participants. Language is capable of serving both cooperation and deception, and under most circumstances serves as a tool allowing common projects to proceed.

We should not, then, be misled by the remarkable capacities language has for mapping and making intelligible; in everyday life, language does not convey anything like a full account of what is going on. That indeed is part of its functional nature; it is one of a number of means actors use to achieve pragmatic ends, so it neglects much that could have been said. A report offers a map through the territory, even though it may be taken by its users as being a sufficient and accurate account for, after all, it allows action.

In practice, as we have seen, reports become actors in their own right; they serve to spread rumours, cause new people to be recruited, and make and break relationships, both informal and formal. In any situation where change is taking place, reports already have gained independence from the situation to which they refer. Language in the form of conversation, overhearing, command, report, even the introduction of a new term, can reveal new relations, participate in change and precipitate further developments.

If this is true under the first scheme, in the second scheme reports become fully independent of sightings and, indeed, do not depend on sightings to have their own validity. In the therapeutic sessions, they develop their autonomous powers by commenting on situations, adding to them and altering their possibilities, and also cancelling previous interpretations and substituting new ways of thinking. In these conditions, speech is no longer part of the linkage of perceptions and reactions, it does not reflect situations, nor does it reveal interactions. It takes on the role of storytelling and constituting new possibilities, saying something that is not the case so that something new may emerge.[18]

At the same time as reports gain autonomy, sightings also alter their powers, requiring to be read by a work of memory and imagination: as we have seen, by observation, thought, recollection and construction. Deleuze claims that visual images under these conditions become 'archaeological, stratigraphic, tectonic', for they reveal the 'deserted layers of our time ... which we juxtapose according to variable orientations and connections' (Deleuze 2005: 234). Certainly, these craft and their occupants mobilize a whole series of levels which we have been doing our best to explore – historical, religious, fictional, political, technical, industrial, technological and so forth. And these explorations in their reported form demand that the reader participate as much as the medium, the operator and the investigator, putting in imaginative effort. In a word, the reported sighting is a form of 'apologetic'.

The sighting then becomes 'readable' just as the report becomes autonomous. Speech no longer accompanies what is seen, which in turn reveals its strata. There is 'a to-ing and fro-ing between speech and image' (Deleuze 2005: 237), a to-and-fro which joins the extraordinary and the

---

18   For these reasons, Deleuze talks about the role of repetitions (which he likens to stuttering) in unorthodox – minority – uses of language, and also points to the unorthodox use of majority languages by minorities and their ability to make new things emerge within the majority language. These abilities give a clue to the contributions small religious groups make to majority culture, the role of millenarian sects, for example, in promoting ideas of equality and democracy. Again, Lepselter (2016) offers material on these lines.

everyday, making new kinds of speech and new structures of space, creating the 'event'. We have two kinds of framing, visual and spoken, and their interactions both generate all the uncertainties and contradictions we have met, the untruths, the revisions, the equivocations between real and imaginary, and act to repair these incommensurable elements, each such act generating new disjunctions.

If incommensurability is the key to these generative moments, they operate only under the condition of the failure of certain second order categories against which we make sense, a (temporary) hiatus in ordering of the first scheme. The new relations that emerge may be contingent and passing or may continue in a new settlement when they become taken for granted (and continuities are discerned by wiser heads between the earlier and later states). We might say that the seer, as prophet, discerns the outline of a new arrangement and contributes to making that new arrangement by that discernment. And while there is novelty in the perceived change (usually rejected at the time by less perceptive people in authority), the seer is not free to conjure up no matter what novelty. The new things perceived both lack much content and serve as relays to break some bonds and make others and to join past times to the present. That is, the novelties perceived and heard (differentially) have a form but little content, or content of an arbitrary kind that does not endure well. They work at a secondary level, the reformulation of compulsions, desires and necessary connections.

V. In sum

What have we learned? In the first place, some general remarks. The subject matter of this chapter is the presuppositions that allow phenomena, both in terms of action and apprehension, and the shifts in these presuppositions in a historical period of large states, industrial scale technology and warfare, hot and cold. These are not linguistic presuppositions, but rather provide the basis on which language constructs its signifying practices. They provide the prior conditions required for making sense, the kinds of images that allow both experience and thought, in this instance, sightings and reports.

Given this focus, the individual is never primary but always threatened by institutions and motives operating at a scale greater than the person, potentially controlled internally by mental suggestion and unconscious influence, and externally by a series of impersonal forces such as the state, financial interests and technology, operating at increasingly vast scales, culminating in an indifferent cosmos. Yet, it turns out, it is possible to experience moments when these overarching schemes falter in their workings, usually by change at one level interfering with the smooth operation of another, and, in these interstices, 'operators' such as flying saucers appear, giving resources for small-scale collective human projects. They allow the past to be surveyed and readjusted and permit the making of new connections, in this fashion sustaining life at a human scale and allowing participants to escape the determinism and reductive nature of the surrounding society, with its banality, consumerism, remote political life, ubiquitous technology and so forth.

These operators exploit shifts in the common order of making sense, when previously efficient schemes suddenly fail to carry conviction, and give access to a different account of reality, so redrawing the possibilities of intervention or, at least, of offering new descriptions and orienting oneself in a new way. In sum, if time is real, producing the new and not just repeating the same, under certain conditions we can see beyond appearances – the succession of pragmatic concerns – to its ceaseless generativity, and – despite initial appearances to the contrary – the modern condition lends itself to these moments of insight.

In more prosaic language, we have learnt, first, that there is a range of possible positions, made up of overlapping sets of presuppositions, a scale of forms that in large part borrow their self-evidence and rightness of fit from scientific work and commitments. And second, that this spectrum of forms is organized around two poles, which may be identified by a number of oppositions depending on the perspective taken: as realism or idealism, as made intelligible by material causes or by mental acts, as an objective or a subjective approach, as confronting a fixed (objective) world or participation in the changing world, as an attitude demanding action or description, or as the transfer from seeing the things in front of one to 'seeing things' drawn from the imagination.

Our interest in these polar types and the variations that lie between them is principally as styles of narrative, indigenous ways of dividing up and recounting the world, employed in the various reports we have read. Although the question of presuppositions is by its nature 'metaphysical', we are not exploring philosophical arguments, and while philosophers have served as guides, we have sought to describe the resources of different positions found on the ground, taken as distinct ways of mapping the world and the human possibilities it contains. Deleuze, in particular, takes a wide range of material including sociological and anthropological ideas to serve his philosophical ends; we have tried to return the compliment, putting his remarkable texts to anthropological purposes.

Abductions may be only a small part of the materials under consideration and, in some regards, atypical of the wider field of flying saucer sightings. Their prime interest for us is that they make clear the properties of the participatory end of the spectrum. They allow this clarity because they have made the therapeutic session indispensable to the recovery of memories, and this practice in turn reproduces features of the spiritualist and mesmerist traditions from which hypnotism separated itself (see Méheust 1999 I: 76–81). This genealogy allows certain connections to be made and parallels to be drawn, this in particular: the gap between what is seen and what is reported continually generates the effects we have mapped. And this process offers a model which applies to the different kinds of encounter which are the ground of other sightings. In short, abductions allow us clear sight of the mechanics of production that allow flying saucers to act as relays, generating connections and causing separations, in the contemporary world.

Last, we have glimpsed the task of an anthropology of this modern condition, which is to reconstruct these positions as fully as possible, rather than to arbitrate or judge between them, then to describe their local histories as they interact, compete, combine with and replace one another and, finally, to delineate the repeating patterns of emergence and covering over, the family resemblances that pertain between succeeding solutions to the 'problem' of flying saucers. The resources for doing this kind of work are not to be found precisely in the spectrum described, but to one side and the other, in a series of small-scale practices of reading, organizing and interpreting materials.

In these first two chapters, we have followed a scale of forms, a series of ways of modelling things, relations and events. It has become clear that, rather than there being a simple alteration of perspective as one moves along the spectrum, with one position replacing another, elements of earlier positions are taken up and deployed in later ones. The spectrum is not made up of alternatives so much as a series of re-imaginings. This is an effect of the realist pole being the default position; people only turn to the powers of the imagination once circumstance determines that pragmatic considerations no longer serve to make things intelligible. We have gained access to these imaginative powers in the form of the sessions where hidden memories of abduction are recovered, drawing conclusions from published materials. But through this investigation, we have recovered many of the features of the wider range of sightings which have arisen in a variety of settings. This is as far as the investigation goes, to which, in the last chapter, I offer a resumé and review.

CHAPTER 3

Images of elsewhere

What does this enquiry into reports of sightings of flying saucers teach us? We are concerned with *perception* – with sightings and how witnesses make sense of sightings in terms of different kinds of report. And perception is immediately caught up in questions of interpretation. Although he underplays the social dimensions of perceiving and interpreting, Bergson puts the matter clearly:

> In fact, there is no perception which is not full of memories. With the immediate and present data of our senses, we mingle a thousand details out of our past experience. In most cases these memories supplant our actual perceptions, of which we then retain only a few hints, thus using them merely as "signs" that recall to us former images. The convenience and rapidity of perception are bought at this price; but hence also springs every kind of illusion. (Bergson 2016: 33)

We might wish to bracket the word 'illusion', but the point is well made. Perception is a function of memory, with both its individual and collective dimensions, and where there are differing memories, there will be disputes about the resulting images. This enquiry concerns one class of contemporary image, images of elsewhere. I shall look at three areas: first, a summary of the argument that has emerged, second, a consideration of the methods used to reach these conclusions and the principal themes explored and, third, some briefly stated wider observations.

I. Summary of the argument

Taken together, these essays offer a description of a feature of contemporary life and indicates the range of materials that have to be considered. Flying saucer sightings may be regarded as one of a sequence of recurring images, a complex of conditions and ideas which finds social expression at intervals. This complex focusses around tracking disturbances in underlying categories allowing measurement and hence the making sense of novelty, disturbances due to innovation in various sciences and their accompanying technologies but which are monitored in terms of intentional beings, non-human agents who have a concern with the outcome of such innovations with regard to human well-being. We can join the dots between such tracings, beginning from Mesmerism around the end of the eighteenth century, passing through Spiritualism in the mid-nineteenth century and its transformations, including Theosophy in the 1880s, to the genre of science fiction writings in the early twentieth century, then to flying saucers sightings from the middle of the last century and to features of the emergence of the space programme and the contemporary search for extra-terrestrial life and signs of intelligence. Each host phenomenon has a life of its own, to which the image in every case contributes, and although the content of each expression alters, taking detail from the contemporary world in each instance, there is a constancy of basic concerns – a moral vision articulated around innovation in the sciences and technology on the one hand and around spiritual or psychic creatures on the other.

The motive force for these appearances and reappearances is neither primarily economic nor military, except to the degree that investment and warfare each promote scientific and technical innovation that in turn removes previous secure bases for making sense of change. The motive force is then what we may call epistemological uncertainty, a temporary loss of conviction attaching to accepted forms of intelligibility, expressed in a potential for improvisation (rather than in psychological states such as anxiety). The forms in which these efforts at monitoring occur are marked by their mobilizing and exploring oscillations between styles expressing certainty (realism) and styles expressing attention or observation (imagination), when all the participants can do is wait upon circumstances, note fragmentation, and create short-term ways of living through uncertain times by forming alliances with new creatures, creatures who bear the signs of superior civilisations in both their technical and psychic powers.

Flying saucers and their earlier confreres are then an improvised response to the expression of real, if transitory, conditions, a more realistic response, indeed, than the projection of a 'realist' vision onto such unruly circumstances. Moreover, they offer resources. For this reason, the most alert practitioners in the technical zones producing these shifts may have recourse to precisely such ideas to allow them to articulate the problems that arise in realist accounts under these conditions, enabling them to create new possibilities. In this fashion, the experts – military men, technicians, engineers, and scientists – produce and manipulate the images that are emerging.

The characteristics of flying saucers alter greatly over time – we have tracked the major shift between sightings and abductions – but that is what would be expected, for they incorporate contemporary discoveries and priorities continually, changing radically in form as they explore the conditions of their production. At the same time, they show continuity with earlier beliefs: we particularly explored the connections with Spiritualism, Theosophy, and science fiction (in the earlier essays), but should note too that mesmeric forms and practices are repeated in the hypnotic sessions used to gain access to accounts of abductions. In their contemporary forms, they investigate what we might call the psychic condition of modernity, mapping the institutions and politics of the military-technical constellation that is both obscure and omni-present in contemporary life, as well as searching among the fragments of everyday life for new forms of solidarity and the possibility of action. In this searching, persons in other parts of society, ufologists and others, are not different to the military engineers and space scientists, using their improvisatory intelligence, both moral and technical, to find new resources and new ways of working over and above the confines of each local situation.

As this summary shows, three distinct narrative strands emerge from the investigation.

Three histories

First, we have a segment of an on-going story. Flying saucer reports emerged in a post-War, military world controlled by technical values; they were investigated by a unit in Air Force intelligence and gained a certain, always controversial, substance as the 'interplanetary hypothesis' through the employment of a series of scientific techniques. This hypothesis was subsequently found wanting and rejected for various reasons and the unit closed. By that time, the cluster of associated ideas and behaviours, now termed by some the 'extra-terrestrial hypothesis', had gained an independent life and had gone in two directions. On the one hand, it was taken up by members of the public who put sightings of flying saucers to local ends, ends that are often obscure to us, and who thereby became subjected to a range of investigations by civilian organizations and by the press, the form of which investigations developed and changed over time. The motives of the various parties – the military, journalists, witnesses, the investigators – were in practice mixed and their interactions often subtle. This form of life began with the work of flying saucer societies (and their opponents) and ends up in the recovery of hidden memories of abductions. On the other hand, the complex of ideas and expectations also played a role in the margins of the space programme, where a repeat version of the earlier security scenario played out: first, always controversial acceptance of the possibility of extra-terrestrial intelligence, then, for a mix of reasons, rejection of the hypothesis, followed by transformation into new forms and new sites of enquiry. This sequence of emergence, influence, controversy, transformation, and new emergence is by no means finished with; this is a story to be continued. New materials are released from time to time by the Pentagon and the most recent have been the subject of a report to Congress in 2021 (of which, more below).

Then, behind this story, we find another, a backstory which explains many of the characteristics of the flying saucer and lends coherence and plausibility to it. This backstory – of which we have only recorded fragments in these essays – links Mesmerism, Spiritualism and Theosophy with the emergence of science fiction. Mesmerism was a form of holistic healing conceived on the model of Newtonian physics in pre-Revolutionary France, a meditation upon the potential for action at a distance, which crossed the Atlantic in the 1830s and there hit the aftershock of the Second Great Awakening, one of the succession of revivals which shape American identity. In a sentence, Mesmerism – trying to use the resources of a new model of physics to heal people – met evangelical religion. The characteristic of this revival was the rejection of Calvinist certainties and the adoption of a kind of voluntarism, looking to acts of the human will rather than to predestination to explain things, and one of the improvised forms Mesmerism gave rise to in its new environment was the reception of communication from the active spirits of dead persons, focussing thereby on intentional action rather than acquiescence in divine destiny. Communication, however, implies physical means of some kind, and speculations about the fate of the dead – intense because of the falling away of Calvinist accounts – became mixed with new ideas about the conservation of energy and the certainty of continuity between transformed states. The dead were given form in the activities of spirits who employed mental powers discovered through Mesmerism, being allowed in this way to sustain the interests and connections they had formed during their earthly lives; they were able to see the future, travel instantaneously over distances, communicate mentally with each other and the living, and so forth.

The spiritualist movement which resulted showed a progressive development over the last third of the nineteenth century, both in Europe and the United States, and, as an empirically focussed phenomenon, was intimately linked to each new scientific discovery made in this period. For our purposes, the crucial moment was when Spiritualism was drawn into a new synthesis in the 1880s by Madame Blavatsky, founder of the Theosophical movement. Her insight was to identify the extraordinary expansion of scale that was becoming apparent in these discoveries, as understanding developed of geological and evolutionary time, on the one hand, and of atomic and cosmological structure, on the other. It became necessary to understand natural processes as taking place at both far smaller a scale than had previously been conceived and at far larger, and as time being correspondingly both subdivided and extended to cope with the processes being uncovered. Madame Blavatsky's genius was to place spirits as the controlling factors at every level of the newly conceived universe, ordering processes at every scale, whether atomic, terrestrial, or cosmic, and operating in every conceivable time frame. In her synthesis, spirits, with their mental powers of clairvoyance, telepathy, foresight, astral travel and so forth, together with their intense focus on human concerns and wellbeing, were projected onto a cosmic scale: life was distributed into space, they occupied every planet and travelled between them, and intervened in human destiny in many ways, at the personal, race, global and interplanetary levels. This is the narrative of Ascended Masters and Planetary Spirits, but it also integrated smaller, less intelligent sprits – poltergeists, goblins and so on – all gifted with psychic powers and a concern in human lives.

This synthesis was at first confined to theosophical circles but was quickly taken up and disseminated more widely to the newly literate public in the early twentieth century in the form of science fiction and fantasy stories, which was one strand of pulp publishing. Both plots and the powers attributed to space creatures (and to future men) bear out the theosophical influence. In sum, much science fiction is Theosophy transformed. And Theosophy is a liberal Protestant meditation on the fate of the dead, filtered through the new sciences and capable of incorporating new discoveries, such as Quantum Theory and Relativity, without stretching. It is an example of religious and moral thinking with scientific discoveries.

While many of the properties of flying saucers can be traced to experimental technology of the post-War period, this second history explains the values placed on these innovations: the hope of contact with advanced civilizations elsewhere in the Universe, the advanced mental and moral abilities attributed to the occupants of the craft, their interest in the fate of humankind, and their forms of intervention, in many regards resembling ghosts. These ideas also carried with them certain intellectual resources, allowing that mental properties influence material states, so that real world transferences, transitions, and mutations could be thought through in the borrowed categories. Indeed, this intellectual history concerning the invention of the concept of Mind, in parallel with repeated revolutions in the understanding of Matter and its properties, beginning from Mesmerism, allows all kinds of extension, including recourse to science fiction, to mark innovations and expand on the characteristics of various periods in the twentieth and twenty-first centuries. It also points to a second backstory, behind the first.

This third layer is a history both of scientific and technical innovation and of the revisions of patterns of thought that accompany these changes. We sampled this history in the context of the Second World War, showing the link that exists between new weapons technologies and methods of communication, so that radical developments in technical capacity were apprehended in new ways, bringing to the fore the simultaneous appearance of new phenomena and new categories for making sense of them. The reason for highlighting this moment in a much longer history is that it recast understanding of the concept of communication in terms of 'information', formulating the desire for direct, mind-to-mind, contact in a new and persuasive guise. And this in turn allowed a revised understanding of memory as a literal record of the past, capable, even when temporarily forgotten, of being recovered by certain practical techniques without distortion or loss, the discernment of a true signal against a background of noise. This history describes the interplay of a new conception of bodiless communication and recovered memory under the impulsion of constantly developing technologies of recording, storing, and transmitting information. The experience of cinema – watching films – constitutes the commonest form of popular access to this story.

We are concerned, then, with fragments of a history that links changes in technology, communication, and memory, changes in what is achieved, what is conveyed, what is retained, or what can be recorded, transmitted, and replayed. This third history provides the framework for these essays, against which the intellectual background of the second strand (the backstory) and the history of events of the first have to be placed and calibrated.

Yet, the third strand is intertwined with the second, for, over more than two centuries, the history of the properties of the mind and the histories of the physical sciences and their technical outworking have borrowed hypotheses one from another, lent vocabulary, mimicked each other's explorations, and given life to ideas first considered but then modified or rejected by the other. The modern project of defining the properties of mind began from the concept of action at a distance and is tied even now to the aspiration of complete physical explanation for mental acts. Perhaps the most significant feature of that history of mental facts is that it provides overlapping, participatory categories which allow the shifts that occur repeatedly in the history of technology to be mapped, shifts that are otherwise underprovided for by the positivist ambition of using only clear, unambiguous distinctions. In this fashion, the technical history of communication repeatedly provides support for the claims of the 'paranormal' tradition which, in turn, anticipates the mindful forms by which the history of communication advances.

A recent case

However, these three histories are not simply 'stacked' in terms of causal powers, so that shifts in categories allow speculative schemes which in turn permit a series of realizations – events and reports – although we can say that the first history, the sequence of events we have traced, is given form by the interplay of the second and third histories. For, by the end of the investigation, we have identified the smallest social unit, the therapeutic session for the recovery of lost memories, which serves to model the means of producing this interplay of real and imaginary which is the mark of successive technologies of communication; the session allows the investigation of practices that occur much more widely in the history of events, but to which we rarely gain such good access. And, in practice, priority must be granted to the specific conditions, the constraints and opportunities contained in particulars and local contingencies, which control the uses made of the framing narratives. We shall return to the question of starting from particulars in the next section.

For this reason, while we began this enquiry tracing specific descriptions in the distinct areas of the military-technical constellation, the science fiction milieu, and the world of civilian sightings and reports, in so doing we also saw emerge three more general topics, the interpenetration of military technology and media practices, the rise of a certain conception of communication as the unobstructed transfer of information, and an understanding of memory as the accurate and detailed recall of the past: linked topics that provide categories that simultaneously reveal and conceal the underlying processes at work, shaping the dominant narrative that it has been our task to read and comment on.

The much-anticipated release in June 2021 of a US government report on 'Unidentified Aerial Phenomena' (UAPs) (as they are termed in the publication) offers the latest example of this narrative.[1] The report looks at recent sightings of UAPs: fast moving objects filmed by aircraft or from naval vessels, objects which show extraordinary manoeuvrability, and which exhibit intelligent behaviour, apparently investigating ships and accelerating away when approached by aircraft, shooting into the sky or, sometimes, plunging into the sea. The question of their origin is an important one, for they might be supersonic weapons systems produced by other countries, yet their performance appears vastly advanced and beyond any known technology, with acceleration and deceleration powers that would destroy any human pilot. This combination of elements – aerial sightings, political interest for defence reasons, the possibility of extra-terrestrial origins, neither endorsed nor quashed – has been repeated at intervals for the last seventy-five years. Discussions of the report have led to renewed theorising about potential interstellar origins, possible life-bearing planets in other solar systems, the conditions for development of other technological civilisations on such planets, and speculation concerning projects of observation and communication carried out by artificial intelligence – robots perhaps launched thousands of years ago but capable of undertaking research in our locality and in real time.[2] The report, however, is far more circumspect, confining itself to reviewing the evidence but eschewing conclusions about extra-terrestrial origins.

---

1   Office of the Director of National Intelligence, *Preliminary Assessment: Unidentified Aerial Phenomena*, 25 June 2021.
2   See, for example, articles in *The Guardian* 13 January 2021, *The New Yorker* 14 May 2021, *New York Times* 3 June 2021, *Scientific American* 21 June 2021, *The New Statesman* 30 June 2021.

All the discussion shows an underlying concern not only with technological innovation – the latest military hardware and developments in information technology, not to mention the findings of radio astronomy – but also with a certain conception of communication, understood as the central characteristic of intention and therefore of intelligent life, human or otherwise. The communication of information from one mind to another has been central to imagining the purposes and actions of visitors from other planets. Speculation concerning their aims in showing themselves, their possible agenda, what they might be seeking to exchange, and our anticipation of the appropriate forms of contact (the search for signals, construing and constructing alien languages), are all cast in terms of the exchange of information. Without the concept of information and the ambition of its pure (bodiless) communication, we would have no frame within which to make sense of our hopes of encounter. And information – which is a structuring concern of the report – links up with a particular understanding of memory, conceived as the retention of accurate information; the recovery of a particular significant encounter in the past and therefore an accurate record retained with all its significance intact, capable of being re-lived and explored in full. This is memory as film. This idea is needed to give character and purpose to the possible alien visitors, who may be future forms of life bearing an understanding of the past (which, for us, means our future history) and so are able to help guide us through threats and crises. Although the idea of memory has a long history, the concept only gained its present possibilities, that of access to accurate and complete records, recently, with new recording technologies and the focus on the ideal of transparent communication of information between minds. Hence the play with artificial intelligence in satellites, monitoring us and, perhaps, relaying information home.

The basic materials, then, for understanding the continuing life of sightings of unidentified flying objects are confirmed in this latest example. First, the close mutual implication of weapons technology and media images, together with the taking up in these images of theosophical ideas, transmitted through science fiction, of minds 'out there' concerned with human contributions to cosmic evolution. Then, an over-reliance on the ideal of direct communication between minds, taken up and elaborated

Images of elsewhere 97

in the idea that information constitutes a key to the intelligibility of the human and natural worlds alike. And last, a notion of memory as the recall of exact information. These three clusters of interrelated ideas have remained relatively constant, although developing, over the past seventy-plus years. Once this complex was initiated, around the end of World War II, it was inevitable that something like flying saucers would make an appearance in a world exhausted by warfare, dominated by security concerns, and obliged to place its hope of survival in the continuous development of new and extraordinary technologies. The categories still generate UFO sightings of the kind we then interpret as: 'Are they true? Or error? Or fiction?' with the accompanying dilemmas for politicians and strategists responsible for national security and providing material for other experts, commentators and amateur speculators. And the formula has been put to work by the wider population; it has become a key to popular thinking in particular about the centrality of the military-industrial complex to American public life, whether in the ongoing role of media representations that simultaneously display some aspects of that centrality (NASA, for example) and occlude others (such as DARPA: the Defense Advanced Research Projects Agency), or, more generally, in the play of information, memory, and forgetting which appears both in widespread public distrust of the state and in a vast range of therapies, whether concerned with recovered memory or with clearing obstacles to communication with self or others. In short, this complex of ideas is well instantiated in the modern world, part of the fabric of our imagination, continually evolving, but with certain constant features, and the phenomena it brings with it will likewise remain a present possibility.

II. Approach and themes

If we focus on the particular and the small scale, it is because we are primarily concerned not with representations but with alterations 'behind' representations, the closing of one set of possibilities and the emergence of another. This moment of emergence has been termed an 'event', the simultaneous appearance of new things and new categories by which they may be apprehended, a shift in social space. The commonly employed means for making sense – placing a novelty in a set by comparison with other instances or within a recognized narrative – while a necessary part of recounting the event (and therefore part of this enquiry's subject matter), tend to lose sight of the new phenomena, the new appearances, which are best understood as being distinct from the various available modes of representation. Part of the work is then repeatedly to situate and describe a range of explanations rather than to adopt them as self-sufficient, for they in practice obscure features of the non-representational energies with which we are concerned. Yet, some sociological approaches to phenomena such as flying saucer reports repeat the kinds of partial understanding offered by representations; they both derive from such pictures and support them. We have identified instances of these readings as we have followed specific texts, events, and histories, and while these theories – implicit comparisons and narratives – play their part in each situation, they are not sufficient by themselves to make intelligible the events which are our concern. Indeed, events are in part made up of the simultaneous co-presence of incompatible interpretations.

An appropriate sociological approach

The question then has to be asked, what are appropriate sociological means to allow us to glimpse the expressive moments prior to representation? We are not seeking new comparisons and narratives – although, to repeat, these play their part – but offer rather a series of commentaries and supplements which serve both to point up the lacunae in established positions or explanations and to specify better the active properties that emerge in the circumstances with which we are concerned. To this end, we borrow techniques drawn from textual criticism, anthropological studies and historical approaches, particularly in the history of the sciences, which relate to what may be called the power of fiction in the world, in this sense: that, in particular circumstances, what is imagined (or virtual) produces real world effects. In short, we are concerned with the capacity of the human mind to participate in processes of discovery, not only finding but also making new things.

The appropriate methods to identify these elusive moments and their properties emphasize three aspects: the event, conceived in terms of act and apprehension, the play of claim and recognition as the basis of human social life, and the appropriate scales of human interaction. These themes, which recur, play out in various guises such as rival language ideologies, the distinction between prophecy and prediction, the potential for escape from given forms and for recapture, and realism and imagination as competing forms of intelligibility. We are then concerned with repeated mappings of events and the limits of each alternative. We also noted that rival forms, rather than offering a worldview sufficient to every circumstance, are often in practice adopted according to need or the end in view; they not only act to restrict vision but also serve as tools, allowing access to appropriate powers of interpretation and action. And we have found that science fiction constitutes a commentary on these themes and forms, both repeating them and reviewing their strengths and deficiencies.

In outline, this enquiry is constructed around the two forms of realism and imagination, which link loosely to matters of social scale. We began by considering the life of parts of large organizations – the military-industrial constellation, with its engineers, intelligence operatives and scientists, its political dependency for funding, and so forth – and then turned in the second trio of essays to different materials which give access to a more human scale and detail of human interactions. It is worth remarking that, while we can use science fiction narratives to comment on the larger scale of activity, we turn rather to parallels from Mesmerism, Spiritualism, psychical research and the paranormal to illustrate and investigate the smaller scale.

We started, then, from realist presuppositions and explored a series of moments in the history of images from this perspective: the general conditions of the event in question (war, weapons, media, appearances), the kind of content that can be taken up under these conditions (deriving from Theosophy's playing with earlier innovation in the sciences and the accompanying changes in categories), and the moment when flying saucers appear, combining conditions and content in a sequence of reports of phenomena. We then followed the continuing life of these images, their transformations in interaction with other developments in institutions, technologies and research objects, and their traces too in literary recensions and speculations which played a small but constructive part in these histories. The first approach concluded by reviewing the varied types of social logic or styles of thought which can appear even within these realist conventions, acting as a hinge to open up another perspective.[3]

In the last three essays, we then explored further realizations of these images and their various classifications which took place at a smaller scale, outside the formalized pathways of large organizations and so more idiosyncratic in expression, allowing the description of the emergence and work of imaginative powers. We began with the instantiation of an enduring frame of interpretation, in terms of truth, error, or fiction, and then followed the exploration of the third possibility for its productive potential, an exploration which turned the classification inside out, making its elements interact with one another in new ways. To this end, we described, first, the case of an improvisor with panache in this line and then, a series of inventions and transformations by small groups of actors who worked with the unstable mix that had been created. In these three case studies, we move from generalities expressed in polemical exchanges to small group dynamics and then to the minimum social unit needed to allow the doubling of real and imagined roles.

In the first two chapters of the present essay, the focus has been on recurrent change in the presuppositions of everyday thought, a move from a concern with action to a reflective engagement with perception and mental processes. Rather than directly confront the unnameable processes behind the work of representation, we looked at the instabilities in the various styles of capturing and narrating life. We reached a number of conclusions. First, contemporary puzzles such as strange sightings are made sense of with the help of models drawn from scientific thought, running from well-established forms to recent innovations, which together form a spectrum.

Then, the spectrum can be ordered by identifying as its poles or extreme forms, on one hand, the realist style, which takes a stable external

---

3   This review can be found in Chapter 3 of the fourth essay, *UFO Reports*.

order for granted, an order which can be perceived and responded to and which is open to being modified by intentional acts, and, on the other hand, an imaginative style which emerges when the first style fails, which it does on occasion both for internal reasons and for lack of a supporting context. Taken together, these forms allow the logic to appear that explains the anomalous features of the different accounts we have investigated.

Third, the characteristics which emerge from the second position allow two relations to the past to be discerned, quite distinct from the successive acts of the realist position: repeated returns to different levels in the past, which permit the significance given to things in the present to be recast each time, and the identification of a single 'event' which links revisions of relations at different moments of the past into a unified crisis, bringing together changes in understanding, memory and desire. The two relations each allow the other; an actor can move from one perspective to the other and back; together, they offer a different account of time as a medium for life to the first model, one that generates the most puzzling features that have emerged in earlier descriptions.

And last, the hypnotic session associated with the recovery of hidden memories of abduction allows us to track the mechanism bringing together these two relations to the past and, at the same time, the alternation between realist and imaginative presuppositions, and so to recognize the work that recovered memory achieves. In this fashion, it also indicates the kind of minimal social unit that must be at work more generally to create the anomalous features of flying saucer reports. For the kind of situation the therapy session makes clear is also present in the alterations of atmosphere described in Air Force policy, in the development of SETI in the margins of NASA and, repeatedly, in the construction of local encounters and sightings, but never so visibly.

In short, we find a spectrum of forms that express the predominance of the different social logics and, as we move from one pole to the other, prompted by the instability of each successive position, an increasing infolding of time. We may remark in particular on the shift from the assumption of a linear narrative to a concern with the reiterative recovery of the past.

This focus on the powers of the imagination therefore allows making sense of the dilemmas found in the earlier essays, powers which are only hinted at in these materials in terms of anomalies and indirect recourse by stylistic reference to ghost stories or fairy tales and the like, obscured because the account is always at arm's length, controlled by the demands of realist presuppositions. The object of study may be characterized in its most general aspect, then, as changes in mood or atmosphere, conceived to act simultaneously at both the individual and collective level. Such a change may be experienced as a diminishment in potential or as an augmentation in powers, as an inflexion in direction of research or policy, as bureaucratic change or a shift in organizational politics. And these are not easy matters to speak of, because we have need of something other than the materialist or imaginative forms that cover over these moments of alteration, a notion of change, beyond or behind the forms of representation. Certainly, the records rarely name such alterations directly; they are, rather, either ignored or taken for granted.

Language, time, and action

The couple of realism and imagination then both serves as a frame for the whole enquiry and stands as the conclusion to this investigation into these changes of mood, and we have noted the ability of each form to pass into the other (the imaginative nature of realism, the realism of the imaginative approach) or, more precisely, the capacity of each to stand in for the other and swap between regimes in the minimal unit of production. We have also remarked how the imaginative forms are not simply the negation of realist forms but offer an element of overcoming, containing the potential to recognize the limits of representations of any kind. For this reason, Spiritualism and the like serve well as models to think with.

These oscillations between realist and imaginative forms also appear in a number of more specialized themes which recur throughout the investigation, each showing a developing profile as the argument progresses. I identified three such themes in addition to realism and imagination: different presuppositions about how language works (language models or ideologies), different ways of relating to novelty and time (linked to prophecy and prediction), and the work of non-human agents joining different times, places, people and so forth, creating access to new resources and the possibility of escape from closed situations but also, in practice, open to being recaptured and covered over by familiar terms (relays).

With regard to language, we began with realist presuppositions, but saw how rapidly the business of writing new things into existence using objective language in official reports led to the demand that some of the documents be destroyed in response to changes in policy. For, if there is only a single, literal truth, capable of yielding an objective description in neutral language, other versions cannot even be filed and kept for purposes of record. Inconsistencies in this approach appeared more clearly when we considered the notion of 'communication' that underwrote the project of reporting and the multiple possibilities it brought with it, ambiguities which the concept of 'information' both sought to control and perpetuated. The framework of, on the one hand, seeking mutual transparency between minds (or machines) while ignoring material bodies and, on the other hand, fearing that one mind can only ever be opaque to another and that communication breaks down, appears to be a constant of this approach. These ever-present alternatives, symptoms of the desire for communication, were explored through a range of small-scale examples in the later essays, expressed in a set of characteristic forms, repeating patterns containing moral positions, habits of thought, and social arrangements; we analysed these patterns in terms of rhetorical forms – situated attempts at persuasion rather than objective descriptions – which were anticipated in earlier instances of 'occult' thought and, in particular, spiritualist practices.

From the rhetorical perspective, the method of residues is of special interest because it allows the juxtaposition of alternative approaches and the continual adjustment of the boundary between what may be included as reasonable and what excluded. Rather than taking the alternative candidates as mutually exclusive kinds we have to choose between, we need an understanding of language which includes the force of persuasion acting both on self and others in addition to the functions of indicating objects, conveying feeling, and sharing common grounds of making sense.

The second theme focusses on the repeated breakdown of the realist scheme in terms of anomalies of time and motion and the emergence of a rival kind of perception which contains another relation to time. Again, this topic has several aspects. The first is paranoia, a response to the observation that the world works by quite other rules than the simple matching of word and action. We began with its roots in technological change, followed it through some sociological mappings and literary expression, and then saw how it was put to work as part of a spectrum of ways of responding to the given world and of gaining new capacities. The second motif is what has been called prophecy, understood as reading new conditions rather than any notion of prediction based in continuing social and intellectual forms. It is a response to the opportunities presented by discontinuity. The model here is Madame Blavatsky, but she was followed by a range of lesser figures, sometimes closely linked, sometimes more distantly connected. This form of living in the world – responding to local shifts in categories and possibilities – is in turn connected to the power to bring things into existence, based on the simultaneous capacity to see (something of) what is happening and to exploit the shift by joining in new potentials, to make alliances and so forth. I use the phrase 'writing into existence' to point to this human power. This double aspect is repeated in the work of scientific discovery, where new conditions in the world are forged through the work of human intelligence; experimental systems are, in Rheinberger's words, 'machines for making the future' (Rheinberger 1997: 33). This parallel adds authority to the non-standard interpretations of incidents created by prophets and those who follow them, adding to their disturbing properties. The final feature of the complex effects of the breakdown of the standard schema finds expression in the paradoxes of time travel, challenging the understanding of linear succession which forms a central part of the realist position. We find material on repetition, returns to the past, the drawing of different connections with the past, and the generative power of clashes between incompatible versions of the past. We can also, with a reversal of perspective, anticipate visits from the future. Simple notions of succession, identity, causality, and place become more complex, and ambiguities multiply.

The third theme to emerge under these conditions is that of the 'relay', the act of making connection between disparate times (and places). This notion was introduced in the discussion of Theosophy and the role of mediumship in linking the material and spirit worlds, allowing new forms of small-scale political action. Spiritualism, indeed, can be seen as typical of the entire tradition of using action at a distance as a means for moral speculation and thinking through the social implications of scientific advances and new technologies. It allows an integrated understanding of all aspects of a change in the condition of the world, aspects of which are not grasped by the common-sense categories of the prevalent worldview, and which appears therefore with particular force of conviction at junctures when these dominant categories are exceeded by the unintended effects of technical innovation. Although invisible to most 'experts', this integrated understanding may serve as a tool allowing an actor to respond to a real, if transient, shift in social space.

The focus on relays allows us to glimpse the occasional power of marginal positions and of oppositional groups, which sometimes set terms that are adopted by larger scale organizations. In this fashion, the limits and opportunities of the idea of communication, which shares in this same stock of forms, are taken up and expressed in the inner life of some major institutions and permeate the common life of modern society. Under these conditions, the relays – which have little content to fill out a description – may become routinized, technical objects with known properties, although technical objects of this kind also develop and change as the surrounding conditions alter. But their basic properties remain constant: we find a repeating pattern of flight – escape from conventional forms – and recapture, as these energies first disrupt and then become either domesticated within the family situation or put to work in states apparatuses. At the present time, these are the two alternatives: external life forms, embedded in the machinery of intelligence reports, the search for extra-terrestrial intelligence, and programmes seeking the conditions of life, and forms of personal experience, sought through therapeutic techniques for recovering memories of repeated abductions, from which memories a whole scheme of cosmic research and, perhaps, colonization can be inferred. And an entire, if fragmented, picture of modern society can be included in the deduction, with the external forms playing their part. In either case, the images are repeated, but always with the potential to break out, to escape their present limits and make new alliances, linking up with new elements to produce new effects.

III. Some general conclusions

Social anthropology as a method takes a case study, a local puzzle such as an event, a form of life, a ritual, and draws out the description in two directions. On the one hand, it shows how many practices and ways of making sense that appear in the wider society contribute to shaping the event in question, so that the puzzle, rightly construed, represents something of a microcosm, replicating vital aspects of the larger society of which it is a part. Although seeming trivial at first sight, the case study allows us to see the logic at work in the wider order and its constituent relations or, at least, contributes to our understanding that logic. On the other hand, it enables us to see how the small unit contributes to the life of the wider society, both as a form of memory, allowing ideas, concepts, even a worldview, to be stored, passed on, and made operational under the right circumstances, and, more radically, as offering resources, means of overcoming otherwise insuperable obstacles imposed by the dominant social order, allowing new initiatives and achieving non-standard ends.

In the case we have been considering, reports of flying saucer sightings constitute a puzzle which, when read with care, connect to diverse dimensions of contemporary society and make links between them, while, at the same time, permitting initiatives to be taken in a variety of social environments. Together, these connections and initiatives allow us to understand the character and potential of such anomalous forms of life.

At the same time, matters of more general application have come into view. Again, it is characteristic of the social anthropological method that matters of wider application arise out of specific cases; patterns emerge which may serve in other situations, although generalizations often lose force and conviction the further they move from the situation of their origin.

Modern life and technology – five observations

To repeat the summary offered in the Introduction: My thesis is that, in the modern period, with understandings shaped by new technologies, we are bound to find something like flying saucers, with properties that are both real and imaginary, which act as relays between human groups, places, and times, providing new resources and allowing innovation to happen. Can we draw any more general conclusions from the study? I offer five observations which point to wider debates in the contemporary social sciences and humanities. These concern the importance of realism and imagination as forms of social explanation, the role of unproven ideas in the progress of the sciences, the location of creativity in the wider social order and the significance of marginal groups and persons, the ubiquity of liberal Protestant categories and ways of thinking, and the nature of an anthropology of the contemporary world.

1. Realism and imagination

In the first place, the position which we normally adopt without reflection, realism and its variants, is in fact a far more imaginative, even poetic, form of thought than might at first sight be suspected. This is indicated by the range of characters it allows and the different roles and timelines that appear in realist accounts. There is a good deal going on within life as conceived in a technological civilization, far more than the simple relations aspired to by the model of scientific language might allow us to suppose. The other way about, the work done by the imaginative end of the spectrum becomes more prominent once one appreciates its productive activity, its juxtaposing actual and virtual worlds and permitting the processes described, with the emergence of new properties in each party. This is where we can locate the changes in atmosphere which have been our object. In short, realism proves more elusive than might have been expected, and the work of the imagination more substantial; the balance between the two is altered.

2. The role of unproved ideas in the production of reliable knowledge

Then, for this kind of reason, one cannot fully separate the histories of the sciences and their progress from the obstacles overcome and the discarded hypotheses which can be identified retrospectively in a realist perspective. The imagination plays a different role to its typecast part as the generator of 'errors'; unproved ideas play their part in the production of reliable (scientific) knowledge. In practice, modern societies are mixed forms because of the nature of human intelligence, which continually resorts to existing ideas to make sense of new things and, in so doing, creates further novelties, both in understanding and in fact. There is no priority of fact over imagination in these chains. If that is so, we have to face up to the possibility that aspects of big institutions such as high tech, scientific research, the military and the State cannot be held to be completely separate from the forms of ordinary life, from people's commitments and from non-standard literary and other expressions of those commitments. And we need to look in both directions. We might say as a slogan that, in the modern world, 'the sciences are historical and the humanities are technical' (Sale and Salisbury 2015: xxviii).

It could then be claimed, 'without flying saucers, no manned space programme'. A more modest statement would be that Madame Blavatsky made a definitive contribution to the parameters within which the space industry was conceived and has been pursued. For we can say that, without Madame Blavatsky and without her pulp progeny, there would have been no interplanetary hypothesis. And without the interplanetary hypothesis, any notion of space exploration, even as a possibility, would have taken a quite different form. The military might have developed rockets, the better to kill one another, and even earth-orbiting space platforms from which to threaten to do so, but whether they would have undertaken further space exploration for purely utilitarian ends seems improbable. In practice, the interplanetary hypothesis allowed the hatching of the space programme, a successor to various earth-bound big military projects, notably, the Manhattan Project together with the creation of appropriate delivery systems and, later, the deployment of home radar and the development of communications systems to transmit early warnings, which in turn underwrote the emergence of the computer industry. The interplanetary hypothesis played its part in this sequence, as a big, state-funded project was built on these and other technologies, a project not simply focussed on national defence and warfare but on scientific progress and a national horizon of hope for the future. And, indeed, one only has to glimpse the starting point for this enquiry, that the search for extra-terrestrial intelligence is the latest form of seeking contact with disembodied minds, to grasp the force of the moral human imagination at work.

To make this claim is not, however, to predict future events, as to, for example, whether forms of life will be found elsewhere. Precisely, we do not know the potential of the sciences to find new things; all we know is, first, the discoveries will not be along the lines anticipated (they will be new), and second, in making sense of them we will establish continuities (covering over the novelty) while, at the same time, revising past understandings, making new connections, assembling new profiles. New discoveries create new pasts; everything changes simultaneously, outside linear time, and the imagination plays its part in these moments. These acts of imagination are transitory, not readily grasped, and quickly covered over; they may, nevertheless, have effects which persist.

The kind of problems which confront us, then, are technical and not obvious. In the first place, since we are dealing not in representations but in shifts in definitional space, we are concerned with what we may call the collapse of categories. Under stable conditions, we use secure second-order forms of measurement to make sense of novelties; we make sense of new things by placing them with respect to established understandings. But under conditions of innovation, some forms of measurement no longer operate; the behind-the-scenes forms of knowledge no longer hold.

These conditions are transitory, and local, and often spotted only by a few of those involved, but under these conditions a whole series of normal schemes for putting order into things appear to fail. Mostly, they fail around what we may call the axis of time: succession in time becomes unclear; cause and effect become reversed; memory, understanding and desire (or knowledge of the past, grasp of the present and hope for the future) mutate; and the identity of each actor, conceived as a single personality with intentions and emotions, becomes multiplied.

These are the kind of effects that are produced in collective thought through 'discoveries' in the nature of matter such as action at a distance, the law of conservation of energy, non-Euclidean geometries or the Theory of Relativity (looking only to earlier instances). Technologies are one form of improvisation, essentially of a problem-solving kind, that play on the possibilities inherent in matter, and can be conceived (to echo an earlier formulation) as part of a wider set of human concerns about encountering oneself and negotiating one's personal and historical (collective) origins, likewise exploiting the same possibilities to change the terms of self-understanding. As I have suggested, these conditions of disturbance are apparently short-lived; the effects of innovation become mapped again, and the discontinuities can be covered over, and previous forms of making sense resumed – but they may lack conviction and be subtly displaced, no longer forming an unquestioned horizon but now forming one of a series of options, waiting for the next disturbance.

In the second place, under the particular circumstances of category collapse, language takes on a different role. Under normal circumstances, one looks to sentences to perform work of designation, manifestation, and signification: they refer to some object or state of affairs in the world (the 'truth'), they convey the ideas and beliefs in the mind of the speaker, and they evoke the universal concepts on which the proposition depends. Under the exceptional circumstances with which we are concerned, these functions cease to be primary; we can no longer rely on reference, emotions, or universals. Instead, language takes on active properties, sharing in events and the registration of events through the business of construction and definition. Under these conditions, naming may call imagined entities into being. One consequence of these ideas, with their focus on mutability and the shifting of frames of reference, is that we should not have too stable a picture of human nature and of human capacities and qualities.

Images of elsewhere

3. The social location of the production of novelty

Third, on the basis of the case studies, we can suggest a similar circuit in terms of the social location of non-standard ideas. The interplanetary hypothesis originated in a constellation made up of military security, technological industries, university knowledge, and state and private finance. The ideas created in this precise environment escaped and were put to work in other spheres – those of ordinary lives, popular publications, journalism, 'amateur' scientific societies and so forth. Yet, as we have seen, the traffic of ideas and influences ran in both directions, not least in the borrowed grammar of the original hypothesis, and, for this reason, repeated patterns emerged in the different spheres of activity, as the traded forms acted as relays, making and breaking connections and appearing in ghost-like guise, with little content; they were lent, juxtaposed, transformed and put to work in each context, expressing the kind of social logic we have tried to describe. In short, although modern technological life is marked by its vast scale, the dispersal of institutions and the resulting heterogeneity of social classes, each with its own kinds of experience, nevertheless, there are features which recall the sociological concept of a 'total social fact', where these distinct parts impinge on one another and can only be explained by their mutual dependence.

4. Liberal Protestant attitudes

We can go further. On the basis of this account, we can say that liberal Protestant commitments, notions which make us in large part responsible for our own salvation and allow us to contribute to the direction and purposes of the world and, indeed, of the Universe, are to be found everywhere, and in the most unexpected places. This religious mindset – a form of responsible realism – may indeed be the default position held in elite circles in the modern period. In which case, rather than counting congregations or speaking of the influence of religious organizations, to see the modern life of religion we need instead to be looking to the styles of argument, the motivations at work, the basic presuppositions, of our common life. To over-simplify on the basis of a single case, the spirits of the dead, still active, still concerned, shape the budgets and aims of the extraordinary contemporary projects surveying outer space and listening for signals from out there.

However, if these categories and their effects are to be found active in every part of the social order, that does not imply they are effective in any simple causal fashion. Here we are brought to consider the role of what we have called the 'second order' or unstated. For, if humans improvise brilliantly, so brilliantly that they allow new possibilities even to high-tech, state-funded programmes, this is not evidence of their direct expression or authority in these spheres. Improvisations of the kind pointed to happen in 'spaces' that are opened up by the work of the sciences and their technological out-workings, when new discoveries undermine the taken-for-granted order of things, so that basic categories of space, time, matter, force, even cause, mutate and take on new forms, using materials that come to hand. The categories by which we previously made sense of new things, of novelties, become insecure and, in those moments, the human imagination has the power of realizing its ideas: thought can become real and produce material effects. In this perspective, improvisation is not a comforting term: it does not suggest the continuation of known things by other means, but instead implies that human intelligence can produce effects far beyond either its intentions or its control.

5. The anthropological task

At various points in this last essay, I have pointed to what I conceive to be the task of an anthropology of the contemporary world, viewed in this light. We seek to formulate principles that allow us to do two things: to identify the interactions between ostensibly autonomous zones of modern life, taking account of the dissolution of individual initiative in the idea of assemblages of objects and information, on the one hand, and, on the other, to acknowledge the person as the singular point where assemblages interact in moments of creation of novelty, before systems succeed in recapturing the new and putting it to work. The case at issue is a good instance both of dissolution of identity and singularity. An unprovable idea – the flying saucer – is transitory and yet has enduring and widespread effects, remaining curiously active, joining different times and human groups, and allowing new things to emerge, things which cannot be anticipated in advance. It is a point of genuine human creativity.

The social scientist, then, deals not in facts but in meanings and, more, the history of the meanings in question: the successive shifts in focus, the interest that take hold, the underlying means for making sense. There may be no enduring sense in the genealogies we trace, for narrative changes the possibility of action, which feeds back into narrative, in turn altering the rules. We are dealing in ground rules which repeatedly shift in response to the readings they have permitted or, even, provoked, and so with changes which remove any possible continuities of interpretation, whether in what is desired (intention), in the person who acts (identity), or in what is retained (memory).

The task, then, is to find a consistent way of talking about the role reports – rumours, claims, contestation, rapportage – play in creating novelty in the world: 'Verbal constructs alter the political, social parameters of human behaviour ... rhetoric and prophecy can shape the mind to new ... [forms] and acceptances'.[4] At the same time, we have to acknowledge the changes in categories that reports effect can neither be mapped exhaustively in language nor fully accounted for by the appearance of new objects. We are, in short, dealing in signs (for want of a better term) that lead neither exactly to thought nor to action, and seeking to account for the way that humans produce 'life' outside their powers of representation. These transitory moments of production are real, yet cannot be fully represented in their effects, they upset conventions and are misrecognized, and they are apprehended in ways that do not do them justice.

Are flying saucers real?

Finally, are flying saucers real? The answer to that depends on where along the spectrum of styles of interpretation you set the dial, or where circumstances set the dial. You can set it at the realist end, whereupon anomalies

4   Anon (1974: 354).

accrue, and controversies arise, or you can move it to the other, imaginary end, where people depend on indirect evidence and testimony, but where, as we have seen, a good deal of sense can be made. The question of realism is not, in the end, all that important. The key to interpretation – and the only major presupposition – is to take seriously each witness and their testimony, to regard each as a serious player in a moral world, seeking to make sense and produce order. And that is where we began the enquiry.

Bibliography

Anon, a review of Jean-Pierre Faye, *Langages totalitaires* and *Théorie du récit*, *The Times Literary Supplement*, 5 April 1974.
Bachelard, Gaston, *La formation de l'esprit scientifique*, Paris, Vrin, 1938.
Bachelard, Gaston, *La philosophie du non*, Paris, Quadrige, Presses Universitaires de France, 2008 [1940].
Bachelard, Gaston, *La poétique de l'espace*, Paris, Presses Universitaires de France, 1958.
Bachelard, Gaston, *Le rationalisme appliqué*, Quadrige, Presses Universitaires de France, 2004 [1949].
Bender, Courtney, *The New Metaphysicals: Spirituality and the American Religious Imagination*, Chicago, University of Chicago Press, 2010.
Bergson, Henri, *Matter and Memory*, New York, Zone Books, 2016 [Paris, 1908].
Blish, James, *Galactic Cluster*, New York, Signet Books, 1959.
Canguilhem, Georges, *Etudes d'histoire et de philosophie des sciences*, Paris, Vrin, 1970.
Clark, Jerome, *The UFO Book: Encyclopaedia of the Extraterrestrial*, Detroit, Visible Ink Press, 1998.
Clarke, Arthur C., *Childhood's End*, London, Tor (Pan Macmillan), 2010 [1953].
Crane, Tim, *The Objects of Thought*, Oxford, Oxford University Press, 2013.
Cugno, Alain, *St John of the Cross: The Life and Thought of a Christian Mystic*, London, Burns & Oates, 1982 [1979].
Dean, Jodi, *Aliens in America: Conspiracy Cultures from Outerspace to Cyberspace*, Ithaca, NY, Cornell University Press, 1998.
Deleuze, Gilles, *Cinema 1: The Movement-Image*, Minneapolis, University of Minnesota Press, 2001 [1983].
Deleuze, Gilles, *Cinema 2: The Time-Image*, London, Continuum, 2005 [1985].
DeLillo, Don, *Americana*, London, Penguin Books, 2011 [1971].
Denzler, Brenda, *The Lure of the Edge: Scientific Passions, Religious Beliefs, and the Pursuit of UFOs*, Berkeley, University of California Press, 2001.
Faubion, James, *The Shadows and Lights of Waco: Millennialism Today*, Princeton, Princeton University Press, 2001.
Fuller, John, *Incident at Exeter* (1966a) *and The Interrupted Journey* (1966b), published in one volume, New York, MJF Books, 1966.
Hopkins, Budd, *Intruders: The Incredible Visitations at Copley Woods*, New York, Random House, 1987.

Hopkins, Budd, *Missing Time*, New York, Richard Marek Publishers, 1981.
Jenkins, Timothy, 'Fieldwork and the Perception of Everyday Life', *Man* 29 (2), 1994: 433–455.
Jenkins, Timothy, *Of Flying Saucers and Social Scientists: A Re-reading of When Prophecy Fails and of Cognitive Dissonance*, New York, Palgrave Macmillan, 2013.
Keel, John, *Operation Trojan Horse: The Classic Breakthrough Study of UFOs*, San Antonio, TX, Anomalist Books, 2013.
Keel, John, *Our Haunted Planet*, Greenwich, CN, Fawcett Publications, 1971.
Keel, John, *Searching for the String: Selected Writings of John A. Keel*, Andy Colvin (ed.), Point Pleasant, WV, New Saucerian Books, 2014.
Kemp, Earl, *Who Killed Science Fiction? Compleat & Unexpurgated*, Rhode Island, Merry Blacksmith, 2011.
Keyhoe, Donald, *The Flying Saucers Are Real*, New York, Fawcett Publications, 1950.
Kittler, Friedrich, *Gramophone, Film, Typewriter*, Stanford, CA, Stanford University Press, 1999 [1986].
Laist, Randy, *Technology and Postmodern Subjectivity in Don DeLillo's Novels*, New York, Peter Laing, 2016.
Lepselter, Susan, *The Resonance of Things Unseen: Poetics, Power, Captivity, and UFOs in the American Uncanny*, Ann Arbor, University of Michigan Press, 2016.
Leslie, Desmond and George Adamski, *Flying Saucers Have Landed*, New York, The British Book Centre, 1953.
Maclaren-Ross, Julian, *Bitten by the Tarantula and Other Writing*, Paul Willetts (ed.), London, Black Spring Press, 2005.
Méheust, Bertrand, *Science-fiction et soucoupes volantes: une réalité mythico-physique*, Rennes, Terre de Brume, 2007 [1978].
Méheust, Bertrand, *Somnabulisme et médiumnité (1784–1849)*, 2 vols, Paris, Institut synthélabo pour le progress de la connaissance, 1999.
Menzel, Donald, *Flying Saucers*, Cambridge, MA, Harvard University Press, 1953.
Morton, Timothy, *Realist Magic: Objects, Ontology, Causality*, Ann Arbor, Open Humanities Press, 2013.
Pasulka, D. W., *American Cosmic: UFOs, Religion, Technology*, New York, Oxford University Press, 2019.
Peters, John Durham, *Speaking into the Air: A History of the Idea of Communication*, Chicago, University of Chicago Press, 1999.
Plato, *The Republic*, London, Oxford University Press, 1948.
Rheinberger, Hans-Jörg, *An Epistemology of the Concrete: Twentieth Century Histories of Life*, Durham, NC, Duke University Press, 2010.
Rheinberger, Hans-Jörg, *Towards a History of Epistemic Things: Synthesizing Proteins in the Test Tube*, Stanford, CA, Stanford University Press, 1997.

Ruppelt, Edward J., *The Report on Unidentified Flying Objects: The Original 1956 Edition*, New York, Cosimo Classics, 2011 [Originally Doubleday, 1956].

Sale, Stephen and Laura Salisbury (eds), *Kittler Now: Current Perspectives in Kittler Studies*, Cambridge, Polity Press, 2015.

Saussure, Ferdinand de, *Course in General Linguistics*, London, Fontana, 1974 [1915].

Shaver, Richard S., *I Remember Lemuria (1945)*, reprint, LaVergne, Tennessee, 2016.

Simondon, Gilbert, *L'individuation psychique et collective à la lumière des notions de forme, information, potential et métastabilité*, Paris, Aubier, 1989.

Smith, David and John Protevi, *Gilles Deleuze*, Stanford Encyclopedia of Philosophy (online), 2014.

Stengers, Isabelle and Ilya Prigogine, *The End of Certainty: Time, Chaos and the New Laws of Nature*, New York, Free Press, 1997.

Strieber, Whitley, *Communion: A True Story: Encounters with the Unknown*, London, Arrow Books, 1987.

Theobald, Morell, *Spiritualism at Home*, London, E. W. Allen, 1884.

Turner, Frank Miller, *Between Science and Religion: The Reaction to Scientific Naturalism in Late Victorian England*, New Haven, Yale University Press, 1974.

Vallee, Jacques, *Messengers of Deception: UFO Contacts and Cults*, Berkeley, CA, And/Or Press, 1979.

Vallee, Jacques, *Passport to Magonia: From Folklore to Flying Saucers*, Brisbane, Daily Grail Publishing, 2014 [1969].

Wittenberg, David, *Time Travel: The Popular Philosophy of Narrative*, New York, Fordham University Press, 2013.

Personal acknowledgements

I have accumulated a great many debts during the research for and preparation of this series of essays. My thanks are due to all the following:

First, these institutions and the people involved in them who have discussed ideas with me and helped in practical ways: in Cambridge, Jesus College, the Divinity Faculty, and the Department of Social Anthropology; in Princeton, the Center of Theological Inquiry (CTI).

Then, a number of occasions when these ideas were presented in public; among the more significant exchanges, a paper to Cambridge Anthropologists in March 2016, two papers presented during the programme at CTI, 'The Societal Implications of Astrobiology', October 2016 and March 2017, a workshop at CERN on 'Creativity' in June 2018, and a paper given at the Association of Social Anthropologists conference in Oxford in September 2018.

Among those who have discussed ideas with me and offered practical help: in the College, John Cornwell, Rod Mengham and Juliet Mitchell; in the Faculty, Andrew Davison, Alastair Lockhart, Giles Waller, Sarah Coakley and Janet Soskice, together with the undergraduates who took the third year course on 'Anthropological approaches to contemporary religion' and the graduates who shared in my reading group over the years; in Social Anthropology, James Laidlaw, Joel Robbins and Anastasia Piliavsky; in Princeton, Will Storrar, Dick Fenn and Nicolaas Rupke, as well as the participants in the programme; in other places, David Gellner, Dolores Martinez and Beth Singler. I should particularly thank Joel Robbins, who has helped this project through many discussions and fruitful recommendations for reading, as well as those who have helped by reading and criticizing parts of the text, Nick Adams, Paul Dresch, Simon Conway Morris, Alastair Lockhart and Anastasia Piliavsky.

Those who have helped to get this investigation published: Juliet Mitchell, Tim Matthews, Florian Mussgnug and, at Peter Lang, Laurel Plapp and the Production team there, particularly Shruthi Maniyodath.

Also, Piers Vitebsky and Andrew Davison, who put in work on my behalf in this regard, and John Cornwell, who has always been generous with his time, practical advice and useful contacts. As well as these, the anonymous readers at various stages of production, whose input has helped develop the texts.

Finally, there are two groups of people who have accompanied this project over the years it has taken to find form. First, my friends, David Ford, Ben Quash and Nick Adams, to whom I owe much. And then, my family, especially my wife, Diane Palmer, to whom I owe everything; they have assisted the project with encouragement and gifts of books, while my brother-in-law, Ivor Stolliday, has kept me up to date with stories on the Internet and has provided an invaluable service as the first reader of the investigation as a whole.

My thanks to you all and to the many others who have shared in this project.

Cambridge, December 2024.

Index

abductee 47, 62, 67, 74–75, 76
abduction 7, 8, 26, 39, 46–47, 51, 53, 61, 62–63, 65, 69, 75–76, 84–85, 89, 105
action (cf. observation) 8, 25–26, 50, 55, 59, 74, 81
Adamski, George 17, 28–29, 31, 34, 38, 39, 40, 41, 44, 48, 53, 56, 58
alien 11, 16, 30, 37, 48, 52, 75, 96 see also visitor
animism 18
anomaly/ anomalies 31–33, 50, 57–58, 59, 73, 102, 104
anthropology/ anthropological task 71, 77–79, 84, 106–107, 112–113

Bachelard, Gaston 7, 13–23, 73, 78
Bender, Courtney 60
Bergson, Henri 23, 27, 31, 42, 87
Blavatsky, Helena Petrovna 91, 92, 104, 108

categories 4, 7, 10, 26, 33, 40, 79, 92, 93, 94, 95, 98, 104, 105, 113
  second order categories 25, 65, 82, 88, 109, 112
Clarke, Arthur C. 38, 45
cliché 52, 53, 55, 57, 76, 79
Close Encounters 2, 29, 31, 41, 53
communication 2, 27, 30, 32, 35, 38, 44, 48, 49, 74, 91, 93–94, 94–97, 103, 105
communications technology 1, 52, 109
comparison 9–11, 35, 65, 98

confrontation 28, 29, 30, 34, 35, 36, 37
creativity 77, 107, 113

Deleuze, Gilles 27–85
DeLillo, Don 51
description 25, 26–28, 50, 53, 54–59, 71, 72–74, 78, 84, 103
dreams 22, 31, 32, 48, 56, 60, 61, 62, 72, 73

elementary forms 11, 65
empiricism 13, 14, 18
event 27, 33, 37, 41, 42, 43, 49, 50, 56, 65, 66, 68, 69, 71, 72, 73, 74, 82, 98, 99, 101, 110
exchange (of real and virtual) 54, 56, 63, 65, 72, 78

fiction 77–79, 98–99
film 2, 12, 26–28, 31, 60, 93, 96
Fuller, John 45, 48, 59–61, 72

Hill, Barney and Betty 54, 59–62, 69
Hopkins, Budd 54, 60, 62–63, 66, 67, 70–71
hypnosis 21, 46, 48, 54, 60, 61, 66, 69, 71, 74, 75, 76–77, 78, 89, 101
hypotheses, discarded 19, 21, 108
hypothesis, interplanetary 90, 108–109, 111

image 1, 3, 41, 63, 81, 87, 88
images 57, 65, 76, 77, 78, 83, 89, 96, 99–100, 106

imagination (cf. real) 3, 31, 32, 36, 43, 56, 72, 73, 74, 81, 84, 85, 89, 99, 102, 107–108, 109, 112 *see also* virtual
information 93, 95, 96–97, 103
interval 31, 32, 40, 42, 46–47, 49, 58, 64, 77

Keel, John 16, 17, 39, 44, 45, 46, 53, 75
Keyhoe, Donald 14

language 42, 58, 80–82, 99, 102–103, 107, 110
Lepselter, Susan 53, 66, 76, 78, 81
liberal Protestant thought 4, 5–7, 92, 107, 111–112
logic of events 31, 46, 56, 71

marginal groups and persons 55, 105, 107
medium 54, 61, 62, 65, 70, 74–77, 81
memory 7, 32, 33, 46, 47, 53, 59, 64, 67, 70, 77, 81, 87, 93, 95, 96–97, 110, 113
memory, recovered 8, 46, 60, 61, 70, 93, 97, 101 *see also* recollection
mental powers 16, 21, 22, 38, 91, 92
Menzel, Donald 14
Mesmerism 56, 88, 91, 93, 99
mind and matter 17, 23, 40, 48, 70, 72, 73, 79, 92–93, 94, 99
models, of language 57–58, 80–82, 102
models, scientific 7–8, 9–23, 91, 100
modern life 89, 107–114
modernism 43, 51, 53
multiple personality 69
multiplicity 43, 75

narrative 28–42, 43–53, 60, 72–74, 76, 84, 90–94, 95, 113
naturalism 43, 44–46, 53, 75
nowhere-in-particular 47–49, 50, 53

observation (cf. action) 8, 25–28, 50, 55, 59, 74, 81, 89
obstacle 19, 20, 67, 97, 106, 108
Office of the Director of National Intelligence (report of) 1, 95

paranoia 52, 53, 104
penny dropping 37, 54, 71
perception 6, 10, 11, 15, 23, 25, 26, 31, 32, 40, 42, 47, 50, 52, 54, 56, 64, 69, 72, 81, 87, 100, 104
presuppositions 3, 9–23, 25–85, 99–102
profile 22, 44, 109
prophecy and prediction 73, 99, 103, 104
prophet, prophecy 57, 65, 82, 104, 113 *see also* seer
psychical phenomena 32, 99
psychological explanation 15, 45, 88
psychological warfare 45, 52

rationalism 13–17, 18, 19, 22
rationalism, applied 19
rationalism, completed 16, 18
rationalism, dialectical 17, 18, 22
real (cf. virtual) 3, 11–23, 36, 48, 54–66, 71–82, 94, 99, 100, 112
realism 13, 15–16, 25, 33, 36, 37, 40–42, 46, 56, 59, 83, 89, 99, 102, 107–108
recollection (remembering) 29, 46, 59–60, 61–64, 66–68 *see also* memory, recovered
relay 3, 78, 82, 84, 103, 105, 107, 111
report (cf. sighting) 11, 12, 25–85, 80–82, 83, 94
residues, method of 21, 103
Ruppelt, Edward 14

scale, change in 9–11, 12, 29, 36, 45, 58, 63, 79, 83, 85, 91–92, 99–100, 105

Index

science fiction 3, 11, 15, 18, 30, 53, 88, 89, 91, 92, 94, 96, 99
seer 54, 65, 70, 74, 82 *see also* prophet
SETI (Search for Extra-Terrestrial Intelligence) 2, 53, 88, 101, 105, 109
Shaver, Richard 51, 52, 53, 57
sighting (cf. report) 1, 2, 11–12, 25–85, 87, 88–94, 94–97
sign 6, 12, 28, 32, 50, 51, 54, 56–57, 61, 68, 73, 87, 89, 113
spectrum, philosophical 9–23, 26, 83, 85, 100, 101, 104, 107
spirits 56, 67, 74, 91–92, 105, 111 *see also* medium
Spiritualism 5, 54, 67, 77, 88, 89, 91, 99, 102, 105
Strieber, Whitley 41, 60, 63, 74, 75, 76

Theosophy, theosophists 3, 18, 57, 88, 89, 91, 92, 96, 105
therapeutic session 11, 60, 62, 64, 65, 67, 69, 81, 84, 94
therapist 52, 62, 105
therapy 46
time travelling 15, 30, 104

time, accounts of 3–7, 15, 25–85, 101, 104, 109–110
time, as event 22, 43, 49, 65, 66–71, 73, 82, 98, 101
time, as layers of the past 66–69, 70, 73, 77, 81
time, as succession 31–34, 40, 47, 58, 68, 72, 73, 104
time, lost 47, 54, 59–63, 67, 71, 94
time, non-chronological (simultaneity) 41, 43, 57, 60, 64–66, 66–69, 73, 76, 79, 93, 98, 104

UAPs (Unidentified Aerial Phenomena) 1, 4, 95
unproven ideas 107

Vallee, Jacques 39, 45, 46, 53
virtual (cf. real) 31, 32, 36, 46, 47–49, 56, 59, 60, 62–63, 64, 68, 74, 99 *see also* imagination
visitor 17, 28, 29, 32, 36, 37–39, 40, 41, 46, 47, 48, 50, 56, 62, 63, 71, 96 *see also* alien
voice, internal 33

Wittenberg, David 15, 30

Mini Series: Images of Elsewhere
TIMOTHY JENKINS

Vol. I
Flying Saucers: An Introduction

Vol. II
Religion and Science Fiction

Vol. III
Martian Linguistics

Vol. IV
UFO Reports

Vol. V
Alien Sightings

Vol. VI
Images of Elsewhere

www.ingramcontent.com/pod-product-compliance
Ingram Content Group UK Ltd.
Pitfield, Milton Keynes, MK11 3LW, UK
UKHW021323180426
11947UKWH00017B/1407